THE DEADLY AMIGOS

The *Amigos*, a group of Mexican revolutionaries, was being used as a front for Cass Borman's slick rustling operation. Borman's gang was made up of the worst killers on either side of the border. But into this group came someone new. He was young, lean, hard.

Pete Galahad, he called himself. They tried to bully him— at first. Then they became a little afraid of him. There was something of the smell of death about him.

THE DEADLY AMIGOS

Barry Cord

GUNSMOKE

This hardback edition 2008
by BBC Audiobooks Ltd
by arrangement with
Golden West Literary Agency

ISBN 978 1 405 68248 0

British Library Cataloguing in Publication Data available.

Printed and bound in Great Britain by
CPI Antony Rowe, Chippenham, Wiltshire

Peter B. Germano was born the oldest of six children in New Bedford, Massachusetts. During the Great Depression, he had to go to work before completing high school. It left him with a powerful drive to continue his formal education later in life, finally earning a Master's degree from Loyola University in Los Angeles in 1970. He sold his first Western story to A.A. Wyn's Ace Publishing magazine group when he was twenty years old. In the same issue of *Sure-Fire Western* (1/39) Germano had two stories, one by Peter Germano and the other by **Barry Cord**. He came to prefer the Barry Cord name for his Western fiction. When the Second World War came, he joined the U.S. Marine Corps. Following the war he would be called back to active duty, again as a combat correspondent, during the Korean conflict. In 1948 Germano began publishing a series of Western novels as Barry Cord, notable for their complex plots while the scenes themselves are simply set, with a minimum of description and quick character sketches employed to establish a wide assortment of very different personalities. The pacing, which often seems swift due to the adept use of a parallel plot structure (narrating a story from several different viewpoints), is combined in these novels with atmospheric descriptions of weather and terrain. *Dry Range* (1955), *The Sagebrush Kid* (1954), *The Iron Trail Killers* (1960), and *Trouble in Peaceful Valley* (1968) are among his best Westerns. "The great southwest . . ." Germano wrote in 1982, "this is the country, and these are the people that gripped my imagination . . . and this is what I have been writing about for forty years. And until I die I shall remain the little New England boy who fell in love with the 'West,' and as a man had the opportunity to see it and live in it."

THE DEADLY AMIGOS

I

FROM WHERE the Mexican woman stood frozen against the crumbly adobe wall enclosing the well, she could see the butte around which the trail to the border town of Candelaria curled like some dry snake. She could see it if she raised her eyes, but Juanita Malinas was staring with numbed fear at the slim, insolent-faced man inside the doorway of her *jacal*.

He was holding Ramirez, her ten-year-old boy, one hand clapped to his mouth. The other hand held the razor-sharp blade of a hunting knife lightly against the unmoving boy's throat.

"You do as I say!" the man hissed. "Scream when he is close enough for him to hear you—or your *muchacho* will never again run after the goats!"

The Mexican woman nodded mutely. She was a dumpy, shapeless widow eking out a bare living running goats and selling milk and cheese in town once a week. A widow too poor to attract even a petty thief, she still could not comprehend the calamity which had befallen her.

The two men had ridden up to the *jacal* an hour ago, had taken possession of the place and waited until the dust banner under the distant butte indicated that a rider was heading this way.

Now she stared, still not fully understanding, but knowing only that her only son, her comfort and reason for living, stood within a hair of death.

The man holding Ramirez was slim, young and burned dark as Juanita. But he wasn't Mexican. His hair was sandy, streaked by the border sun, and his eyes were gray and stood out against the darkness of his cheeks.

The other one who had led the two saddle horses out of sight behind the goat shed was an Indian—a Yaqui, sullen and stolid and as broad as he was tall. A bandolier crossed one thick shoulder. The carbine he held in his hands was an old German make, a single shot Krag.

The man in the doorway could not see the road, only the woman by the well. But his voice held an ugly threat. "Make sure he hears—"

He broke off, listening. The sound of an iron-shod animal on the hard-baked road reached him in the buzzing stillness. His face tightened. "Now!" he whispered harshly and made a quick motion with his knife.

Juanita screamed. There was real terror in it, shattering the hot afternoon stillness.

Jeff Corrin was on his way to a rendezvous with his brother in Candelaria. But when he heard that scream he instinctively jerked his horse toward the *jacal* baking on the desert flat. Against the vast emptiness of the border wilderness the *jacal* had been hardly discernible and he'd paid no attention to it.

10

Now he saw the woman standing by the well, holding her hands to the sides of her face. She kept screaming. . . .

The ex-Ranger's eyes made a quick survey of the yard, noting nothing amiss. But something must be wrong, he thought, for this woman to scream with such agonizing terror.

He rode into the yard and pulled up a few feet away. The woman did not look at him, nor did she quit screaming until he slid out of saddle. Jeff's horse stood between him and the door of the adobe hut.

"*Señora*," he said quickly. "What is wrong?"

The woman had ceased screaming. She stood against the well lip, her eyes closed. Her mouth seemed working in silent prayer. Then she made a motion with her hand, into the well.

"My boy, *señor* . . . he fell. . . ."

Jeff moved toward her, concern quickening his step. "I'll take a look—"

He saw her eyes open and fix on the door behind him and a warning rang sharply in Jeff Corrin's head. A mother who had just seen her son fall into a well would be more frantic, more concerned with the boy's immediate plight . . .

His big steeldust snorted warningly. Many times in the past the stallion's keen senses had alerted Corrin to hidden danger . . . he reacted now to the animal's warning with the quickness of a jungle cat.

He spun around just as a small boy hurtled out of the doorway to fall on his face in the yard . . . and then he caught the glitter of sunlight from the knife as it spun toward him.

Jeff's gun was already nestling in his right hand as he turned; he fired once at the knife and it disappeared. His second shot caught the slim gunman dragging at his holster gun.

The man screamed and fell back inside the *jacal.* The woman broke away from the well and fell across her son who lay quiet, sobbing loudly.

From the shed a carbine blasted heavily. The slug chipped adobe from the well rim, screamed wildly off into the desert emptiness.

Jeff caught sight of the squat Yaqui just before the man ducked behind the shed. He made a run for the flimsy structure, skirting the well. A goat, frightened by the gunfire, lunged against its tethering rope, bleating with terror.

Horses blew heavily. Jeff was just rounding the shed when they broke away, stirrups flapping, kicking up dust in wild flight.

The Yaqui almost caught Corrin with that trick.

But the fleeing horses caught Jeff's attention and he stopped, and only the blur of movement along the base of the shed saved him. He lunged aside and ducked and the reloaded Krag air-whipped a bullet past him; then his own Colt emptied in a staccatto burst.

The Indian twisted like a headless rattler; he dragged himself a few feet along the shed before collapsing.

Jeff walked up to him and eyed the still figure. Nobody he'd ever seen before. The silence held only the bleating of the goat and the softer sobbing of the frightened boy.

Jeff walked back to the yard. The woman was on her knees now, holding the boy to her and rocking him gently.

Jeff waited, his narrowed gaze studying the dismal scene: A squalid Mexican *jacal* in the middle of a lonely desert plateau. Two men he had never seen before waiting to kill him.

He knew that this woman and her son had been nothing more than bait to bring him here; he understood the reason for this, too. For at least twenty miles along the trail he had come there was no place where an ambusher could have concealed himself close enough to insure his mission.

He knew this, but not the reason for the ambush. Unless it had to do with his brother, waiting for him in Candelaria.

But no one was supposed to know that he was to meet Texas Ranger Ben Corrin in Candelaria today. No one except Ben.

He bent over the woman and put a gentle hand on her shoulder.

"Is the boy hurt?"

There was something in Jeff's voice that drew the woman's attention. She looked up, her leathery features still frozen in a mask of fear.

She saw a young man, sun-browned and blue-eyed, standing over her—a lean, quietly smiling man with a dimple in the middle of his chin and a strange glint

13

of recklessness in his gaze. He was dressed no differently from the killer who had held a knife to her son's throat, but she saw the sympathy in his face and she reacted to it.

"They made me do it, *señor*. They came an hour ago. Ramirez was with the goats. They brought him to me." She shook her head, not comprehending. "I am a poor widow—I have nothing. I told them. They said they wanted nothing of me. They said they would give me fifty pesos if I did what they wanted. I was to scream when you rode by . . ."

Jeff nodded. "Well, it's over," he said as the woman started to sob again. "No more harm can come to your boy."

He walked to the *jacal* and looked down at the dead man. He looked like some range rider who had just taken off his chaps and come to town for a few drinks. Two fancy, pearl-handled guns in tooled leather holsters were the only odd note; most punchers couldn't afford belt and guns like that.

A tough-looking American and a Yaqui border thief; they made an odd combination. They didn't make sense, either, he reflected—unless they belonged to the outfit that was stirring up all that trouble in Chihuahua.

Jeff thought of his brother waiting for him in Ansara, a whistle stop flanking the tracks of the El Paso & Chihuahua Railroad Line.

He bent and, struggling, picked up the dead man and carried the body behind the shed where he dropped it beside its companion. Then Jeff walked back to Juanita.

"I'll see that someone in Ansara is notified," he told her. "Someone will come for the bodies and bury them." He touched the brim of his hat to her. "*Buenas dias, señora. . . .*"

The big horse snorted as he mounted. He turned the stallion away from the *jacal,* put it to a run toward the down below the distant rim.

His brother was waiting for him in Ansara. But Jeff had the ominous feeling that Ben already was in trouble.

II

"You ARE waiting for someone, *señor.* I see it here, in the way the sand lies . . ."

She was an old crone, a bag of bones rattling inside a brown, wrinkled skin. Her eyes were black shoe buttons, peering through brown paper lids.

Ranger Ben Corrin's big square hand rested on the table in the cantina. He frowned now as the fortune-teller poured more desert sand into his palm and blew on it. She traced the tiny ridges which formed there.

"I see this man, *señor.* Riding a big horse. A man who laughs with the devil in his eyes . . . a handsome man. Younger than you . . . he is a close friend . . . of the same blood, perhaps . . . ah, yes . . . he is your

15

brother. He has been in trouble recently . . . with the law . . . and you sent for him. . . ."

Ben Corrin's palm trembled. Sweat beaded his upper lip . . . he eyed the old crone with narrowed gaze. "You see all this in my palm, old one?"

"In the lines of the sand, *señor*—the grains do not lie." She poured more sand into his palm and blew again. "I see—" Her lips sucked in sharply over worn gums. "The sand, *señor*. I am sorry—"

"What else do you see?" Ben demanded. Despite himself he was intensely interested now. He had assented to this old crone's reading while waiting in the cantina where he had just finished his dinner. He had time to kill in this small border town until Jeff arrived.

How had this old Mexican woman known that his brother was riding to meet him here? What else did she know?

"The sand, *señor*," the woman muttered. "It does not reveal itself. Perhaps another peso—?"

Corrin thrust an American half dollar into her fist. "What else, old one?"

She blew gently. She was humped over his palm, sharp bony shoulders jutting up, clothed in black, so that they looked like crow's wings.

She drew away, clutching her *rebozo* closer around her. She glanced toward the door.

"What did you see?"

"Another rider," she mumbled. Her voice was almost indistinct. "He does not look like a man who belongs here—he is dressed differently, *señor*. He will ride from the south. Soon. And he will ride to the place where the long wire runs along the iron road—"

"The telegraph office?" Ben's voice held a strained wonder.

"Si, *señor*. He will come to this place and he will send a message. To someone far away. And you will speak to him, *señor*—I see it all here, in the grains of sand. You will speak to him and show him what you have in your pocket. And he—he—" She jerked her hand away and the movement spilled sand from Corrin's palm. She stood up, clutching the *rebozo* close around her.

"I cannot see the rest—the sand doesn't blow right. But, *senor* . . . do not bother with this man. Do not talk to him—"

"Why?" Corrin's tone was rough. Tension made the food he had just eaten lie heavy in his stomach. "Why shouldn't I see this man?"

She moved away. "I—I do not read more, *señor*. Only the warning. Do not interfere with this man—"

Ben Corrin stood up, but the old crone was already at the door. He sat back, conscious of the eyes of the round-faced proprietor on him. His hand trembled. He forced a smile to his lips.

What will Jeff say, he thought, when he tells him? Tough old Ranger getting all shook up because some hag blew sand on his palm and warned him!

But how did she know?

He got up and walked to the door of the cantina, his gaze narrowing to the glare of the sun on the sandy street. He waited, leaning against the adobe wall. Unshaven, sandy-haired, blocky and of medium height, he didn't look much different from the others who walked the streets of this border town. Ansara was no more than a huddle of shacks in the desert. One was the depot and telegraph office, squatting by the iron rails that ran without a bend into the low, sage-stippled hills to the northeast—a place where the train stopped only on signal and where a freight car was detached perhaps once a month.

He put a Mexican cheroot between his teeth and lighted up and waited. He had wanted his brother here with him—he knew how close to the edge of lawlessness Jeff was standing.

A jury had found Jeff guilty of justifiable homicide. It turned him free, stripping him only of his Ranger badge. But it would be a long time before the bitterness within Jeff healed.

Ben sighed. If he could get Jeff reinstated as a Ranger—if he could get Jeff to work with him on this dangerous assignment he was on—it might ease the wildness in his younger brother.

Ben saw the rider now as he came up out of the arroyo just beyond the tracks and his thoughts steadied on the reason he had come to Ansara. The horseman wavered in the brutal midday heat, so Ben Corrin could not make out details. Still, the man did not have the appearance of the usual border rider.

Ben's teeth clenched hard on his cigar. *Briscole!* He

18

had not expected this man to show so soon—had not expected him until tomorrow!

The rider was headed straight for the telegraph office. The words of the old fortune-teller echoed in Bens ears.

Do not interfere with this man!

He couldn't let this man go. But there was cold sweat on Ranger Corrin's brow as he pushed away from the cantina wall. It was five hundred long yards to the small depot.

He glanced once toward the north where a brown ribbon of trail showed among the near hills. Jeff would be riding that trail. But the road was empty as far as he could see.

The rider had dismounted and was walking to the telegraph window when Ben mounted the steps to the loading platform. The newcomer was taller than Ben by a head—a heavy-shouldered, handsome man with a clipped military mustache and bright blue eyes. He was at the window, thrusting a sheaf of handwritten papers through the window.

"I'm Roger Briscole," the man said. "Special correspondent for the *New York World*. I want this sent collect to Editor David Hall—"

He turned as Ben approached. Briscole was wearing a white shirt, stained from desert riding, and sand-colored whipcord britches. His black string tie was unknotted, the ends trailing down his shirt.

Ben said coldly, "Mr. Briscole?"

The man nodded, frowning.

"Come with me, please."

Briscole's eyes narrowed. "Just a moment, sir. Who are you?"

Ben Corrin slipped his left hand out of his coat pocket. He held his badge briefly to the other's gaze.

"I want a word with you," he said quietly.

Briscole nodded. His face was dark burned by the sun. He showed only a polite interest. "Why, of course, Ranger."

He walked along the length of the platform with Corrin. "I'd like to lead my horse to wherever you're going?"

Corrin shrugged. He didn't see a gun on Briscole, and if this man was who he claimed to be, he wouldn't be carrying one. But Ben was certain that he was not the *New York World* correspondent.

He waited on the edge of the platform while the Ranger went down the steps and picked up the reins of his cayuse. The sun beat down over the iron rails, sending heat waves shimmering. There was a small movement against the base of a mesquite clinging to the edge of the arroyo from which the rider had come. But Ben Corrin didn't see it.

Briscole hesitated on the platform, smiling down at Ben. "Hot," he said. He reached up and pushed his cream-colored Stetson back on his head.

The rifle bullet from the arroyo hit Ben high in the side, jerking him around. He made a grab for his holster gun but the second shot knocked his right leg from under him. He fell heavily and rolled against the platform and then lay still.

Briscole swung into the saddle of his waiting horse. He was dipping down into the arroyo, three hundred yards away, when Bob Callings, station agent and telegrapher, came running out to the platform.

Ben Corrin was still breathing when the station agent jumped down beside him. Ben was trying to get up, spitting blood. His voice was a half sob of pain and rage: "Get me inside, Bob. I—I need a pencil and paper . . . it's important. . . ."

A half dozen Mexican townsmen straggled up, their movements cautious. It was generally unhealthy to investigate too soon the source of gunshots.

Callings turned to them. "Give me a hand with him, Juan. Lopez, run over to Ladetto's house. Fetch that horse doctor pronto, if he ain't too drunk to walk!"

They carried Ben into the station, laid him out on a bench. He fought off their attempts to make him lie down. "Pencil . . . paper . . ." he snarled. "Got to write something down . . . something for my brother . . . Jeff . . ."

Callings shrugged. He and Juan helped Ben to the nearby desk, sat him down. Callings brought out some paper and a pencil.

They stood by while Ben Corrin wrote. The Ranger paused, his eyes clouding, fighting the pain tearing inside him.

He finished, folded the paper. He beckoned to the lanky station agent. "Rider will be coming to town

21

soon . . . 'fore sundown. My brother—Jeff. See that he gets this . . ."

Callings nodded. "Better rest now." He and Juan brought Ben back to the bench, laid him down.

Ben muttered: "It's important . . . tell Jeff . . ."

Callings walked to the door, looked out. What was keeping Ladetto?

Across the barren flats, in the distance, he could see the faint dust banner of two riders heading for the low, desolate hills of Chihuahua. He shook his head in bewilderment.

He walked back to his desk and picked up the message Roger Briscole had given him. It was an eyewitness account, a special report to the *New York World* concerning the activities of the Mexican revolutionary band that called itself *The Amigos*.

Callings read the story. *Amigos, hell!* he thought sourly. Border killers would be the better name for them. But the *World*'s special correspondent was calling them Mexico's hope for the future.

He turned as a short, swarthy man in rumpled clothes came inside, trailed by several townsmen. Ladetto was primarily a veterinarian, but he treated human ailments as well. He walked over to Ben, frowned, put the back of his hand against Ben's open mouth. Then he turned and looked sharply at the station agent.

"*Señor*," he growled. "This man is dead."

III

Jeff Corrin came to the town of Ansara at sundown. Bob Callings was waiting for him on the depot platform; he had been waiting for Ben's brother to show up a long time now.

He walked to the middle of the sandy road to meet him.

"Jeff Corrin?"

Jeff edged his horse aside and studied the lanky, shirt-sleeved man with the green eyeshade. Then his glance flicked to the small group of men waiting just beyond, in front of the Cantina.

He knew then that something had happened to Ben.

"I'm Jeff Corrin," he acknowledged.

"Man inside my office said to wait for you," Callings explained. His voice was respectful. He had seen a lot of men in his time here; most of the riders who came through Ansara were a rough, dangerous breed. This man was like them, and yet not like them—there was a hardness in Jeff that went deeper than mere bone and muscle.

He's dead," Callings went on. "But he said to give a rider name of Jeff Corrin this message . . ."

Jeff dismounted and took the folded paper from the station agent and read it. He read it slowly, his face revealing nothing to the watching men. Then he folded the paper, tucked it into his pocket.

"I'll take a look at him."

They went inside and Jeff stood by the blanket-covered figure for a moment before reaching down, lifting a corner from Ben's face. He glanced at the still features, then dropped the blanket. He slowly made himself a cigarette.

He and Ben had always gotten along fine although ten years had separated them . . . he had grown to manhood looking up to his older, more amiable brother.

Go ahead, get married, kid, Ben had told him once. *It'll make a man out of you!*

Ben had laughed as he said it, but he had been serious. He was married himself, and the father of three children, all of whom adored Uncle Jeff.

Then Jeff had taken up with a girl . . . a farm girl name of Ellen Larkin. They had planned a wedding . . . it had been a Saturday night . . . and that was the last time Jeff saw Ellen alive.

Two men had ridden by the farm, killed Ellen's father and mother, raped Ellen and left her to die. They had done all this for forty dollars—all the money the Larkins had in the house.

Jeff had just been recruited as a Texas Ranger. He trailed the two men. And killed them. As an officer of the law his job had been to bring them back for trial . . . it was not within his authority to act as judge and executioner.

The jury had been understanding. Captain Hawkins

at Ranger Headquarters had been less forgiving. A martinet, he did not want a man on his staff who forgot he was wearing a badge.

It had not mattered much to Jeff then, turning in his badge—it did not matter much now. But Ben had wanted him back . . . and now, looking down at his dead brother, he felt he owed Ben that much.

He went to the message counter and wrote out two messages. One was to Ben's wife, Lottie. There was not much he could say to his sister-in-law . . . his words of sympathy had a hollow sound.

He sent the other message to Captain Hawkins, Texas Ranger Headquarters.

Then he questioned Callings as to what happened.

"Man named Roger Briscole came to the window to send a wire to New York," Callings told him. "Said he was from the *New York World,* a special correspondent. Then your brother came in . . . they walked out together. I was getting ready to send the story to New York when I heard the shots outside."

"You didn't see who killed Ben?"

Callings shook his head. "He rode into town alone, that Briscole fellow. But when I came out there were two riders heading south. They were quite a ways off, but one of them was Roger Briscole."

Jeff was still a moment, his eyes hard, thoughtful. "That newspaperman's story—you still have it?"

The station agent nodded. "Some tripe about that band of Mexican revolutionaries, the *Amigos.* Sounds like this Briscole fellow is riding with them. He sure paints a pretty picture of those damn killers, if you ask me . . ."

Jeff read the story. Callings was right. If anyone believed this story, then *Vincente Avilla,* the rebel leader, was a kind, patient man anxious only to lead his peasant people to the promised land. A great man of noble intention, centering on liberty and peace . . .

He tossed the story back on Callings' desk and went out.

He was in the Cantina, having a drink, when Captain Hawkins' answer was delivered to him.

The message was blunt.

"Sorry about Ben. We will handle burial. Can't comply with your request for reinstatement as Texas Ranger. My advice—don't go into Mexico. Stay out of trouble.

Jeff crumpled the telegram in his fist. He brought out Ben's scribbled note, read it carefully.

He left Ansara before the moon was up . . . he rode south, into Mexico.

IV

THE DESERT SUN cracked the dry and broken land and the hills were hot and stony. The air clung to Jeff, encasing him as in an oven . . . he paused and eased his saddle and rifle down and spat a thin dry spittle that left no impression on the burning ground.

A horned toad looked up from the shady protection of a small rock. Beady eyes stared briefly at him, then the lids hooded over . . . he crouched motionless, a relic of life from the past.

"You said it," Jeff muttered. He straightened up and looked toward the hills, squinting against the glare of the sun. They seemed utterly barren, absolutely lifeless.

There was no trail of any kind leading this way . . . yet Jeff knew there was a spring and a small stone shack just beyond the butte with the massive overhang of rock and the wind-tortured juniper sprouting from the top.

His brother had learned this much about the *Amigos*.

Jeff glanced back the way he had come. He had sought the hard places, the rocky stretches where his boots left no visible prints—he did not want to be backtracked.

He pushed his hat back on his head and wiped his face with the back of his sleeve as he looked around. He made his glance casual, like a man who's undecided which way to go. He unslung his canteen from his shoulder, shook it. It was almost empty—this part of his deception would be real, he thought, and finished it off. The water tasted dry—it slid down his throat without wetting it . . . it was gone and not even the memory of it was wet.

Jeff picked up his saddle and started to walk toward

the butte. He knew he was being watched—he felt the skin at the back of his neck prickle and his eyes hooded. He had the sudden, sick feeling that his life was hanging on the pressure of a trigger finger—it was being weighed in the watcher's mind, and he was powerless to influence it or affect it.

He kept walking, however, like a man who is lost and completely unaware of anyone within fifty miles. He rested several times—and this was no act, the tiredness with which he sank down.

A half hour later he passed through a gash in the long butte and followed a desert runoff whose dry bed was thick with rocks washed down from above. Spiny shrubs clung to the reddish banks. He followed this until he came to the crest and looked down into a small pocket amidst the burning hills.

To Jeff it was like looking into a cool, clean land. Even the air felt cool. There was green down there, feathery cottonwoods, a stone hut and stone corrals. A dozen horses were bunched together at the north end of the corral, seeking the shade of the pepper tree arching like a green umbrella over them. He saw a bird flit among the green and it was the first sign of winged life Jeff had seen since morning.

He heaved his saddle across his shoulder again and started at a faster pace down the slope, heading for the pool of water he glimpsed between the trees. Reaching it, he sank down and ducked his head into the cool water—he raised his head, then, and sloshed some of the water down his back.

Then he drank, cupping the water in his hands.

He heard the low *whoosh*, an animal sound low and savage in a shaggy throat, and he came up and around just in time to meet the spring of a big, wolflike dog.

The dog came for his throat in a silent, deadly leap. Jeff swerved and cuffed it on the side of its head, a panther-quick blow that slammed the animal down hard on the spongy ground. The dog scrambled up and leaped again and this time Jeff caught it under the shaggy throat and whirled it around, sending the seventy pound animal into the pool.

He waited, his hand on his Colt butt, watching the dog start to paddle for the shore.

"First time any man ever handled Wolf like that," a voice said. It was a nasal voice—it had the quality of disuse in it.

Jeff turned. A gaunt, shabby man in faded bib Levis and dirty underwear faced him. He carried a rifle in his right hand, held carelessly . . . he was a sun-dried, sinewy slab of a man as tall as Jeff. His face was like the land, too, brown and eroded and stubbled with a peppery beard—his mouth was slack and tobacco juice stained his chin.

Jeff glanced at the hut. "Your place?"

The gaunt man nodded.

"I want to buy a horse." Jeff kept the corner of his gaze on the shaggy dog, who had emerged from the pool and was shaking himself dry.

"Ain't got none," the gaunt man said. He didn't move from where he was standing.

But the dog crouched now, began to move toward Jeff on his belly.

"Your dog?" Jeff's voice was hard.

"Yup."

"Tell him to behave, then. Or you'll lose him."

The gaunt man considered this. Then he nodded. "Wolf!" he called sharply. "Git back to the house. Git!"

Wolf growled rebelliously. But he got up off his belly, backed off, then turned and went loping toward the hut.

"I counted a dozen cayuses from the top of the hill," Jeff said.

"Ain't got none," the gaunt man repeated calmly. "None for sale."

Jeff's eyes narrowed. "I'll give you a hundred dollars for the worst one in your corral—"

The gaunt man's eyes glittered with sudden greed. "Might consider it. How much you got?"

"The hundred I offered you, no more!"

The gaunt man cackled. "Hear him, Jack? He's talkin' tough!"

A shorter man came into Jeff's sight now, pausing by one of the cottonwoods. He was younger and wiry and a good deal cleaner—he had recently bought a gray hat and new boots. The gun in his right hand was new, too—or the muzzle had been recently blued.

"You want a horse?" he asked. "Why?"

Jeff eyed them both—he saw that he was whipsawed between them—the gaunt man with the rifle and the younger one holding a Colt.

"Ran into an Apache war party," he said. "They killed my horse."

Jack's eyes narrowed. "Medano's tribe has been shut up in Fort Gower for two weeks, pending an investigation. Ain't been an Apache off the reservation within ninety miles."

Jeff shrugged. "Would a posse suit you better? A bad fall—a broken leg?"

Jack sneered. "It might."

He made a motion with his gun. "Fancy looking hardware for a down-at-the-heels drifter. Take your gun out slow and toss it to me."

Jeff hesitated.

The gaunt man said: "The kid ain't foolin', mister."

Jeff shrugged. He started to reach for his Colt—then his hand blurred and there was a puff of smoke at his hip and Jack's hand jerked as his gun spun out of it.

Jeff swung sharply, his muzzle targeting the gaunt man. The older man dropped his rifle.

Jack stood still, his lips curled, half in pain, half in unbelief. His hand bled from the bullet gash across his knuckles.

Jeff said coldly: "I'm still willing to pay a hundred dollars in gold for a horse. But now I'll want the best you have in that corral—I'll pick him out myself!"

There was a long moment of silence. Then a voice from beyond Jeff said: "Let him have a horse, Phineas."

There were a half dozen riders just beyond the trees behind Jeff, waiting there as though they had formed out of thin air. Five of them were men. The sixth was a girl.

She was young, strikingly beautiful, blonde—a startling contrast to the men she rode with. She studied Jeff with little interest . . . there was a cold arrogance in this girl that put her above her surroundings.

The man beside her was lean and hawklike, about forty . . . and with a dusty, frayed brush jacket crossed by cartridge bandoliers. He had bright black, restless eyes in which burned a bitter cynical fire. He wore an anthill hat, thus deliberately setting himself apart from the four men with him . . . he was Mexican and they were not, and yet—without making a move or saying anything—he dominated them, overshadowed them.

He leaned forward over his saddle horn now, a faint smile on his face as he looked at Jeff. His hands were small, brown, quick—they gave the impression of quickness even in repose.

"Not many men find their way to Escondido Valley, *amigo*. What brings you here?"

Jeff still had his Colt in his fist, but he knew he'd be dead if he made a wrong move with it. Very slowly he eased it back into his holster.

"You have not answered," the Mexican said. There was a threat in the softness of his voice and Jeff knew without ever having met the man that he was looking at Vincente Avilla. He was not what Jeff had expected. This was no uneducated peon with a drive for power, using the time-worn cliché of freedom for the common people of Mexico as a leverage to political power.

32

Nor were the men with him Mexican. They were Americans—gun-handy adventurers whose only allegiance was to gold, Mexican or otherwise.

"I lost my horse back on the desert," he said. "I just started walking—"

"And stumbled on this little valley, my friend?"

"Yeah—lucky for me," Jeff nodded. "Spotted those horses in the corral—" He shrugged. "I'm headed for Vera Cruz."

Vincente Avilla leaned forward over his saddle horn. "Vera Cruz, my friend, is a long way off. And these are troubled times in Mexico."

"So I've heard."

Avilla glanced at Phineas and Jack; he seemed to be judging something in his mind.

"I am Vincente Avilla," he said to Jeff. "You have heard of me?"

Jeff nodded. "Good and bad. You are the boss of the *Amigos.*"

Vincente eyed him. "Their leader," he said coldly. He turned to the man next to him. The man's left ear was missing, only a misshapen lump of flesh where it had been. He had a steel wire body under dusty clothes, and a young but incredibly ugly face.

"This is Silent Gordon, my *segundo.*" There was a faint mockery in Avilla's voice now. "Silent is a lover of freedom—a deadly enemy of Mexico's oppressors." He pointed to the others with him: Nogales Smith, a runty, balding man with blue eyes in a round, almost cherubic face. He had a limp cigarette in his mouth. Nat

Hines was a stocky man who looked like an unsuccessful rancher. Cob Eaton was taller, with emotionless features. All of them were heavily armed, deadly.

"And—my niece, Maria," Vincente concluded. He looked at Jeff, smiling. "And you—my friend—who are you?"

"Pete," Jeff said . . . "Pete Galahad."

The girl stirred and interest quickened in her eyes. Vincente scowled. "Galahad?"

"You want a name," Jeff said. "Galahad's as good as any."

Vincente studied him, his eyes narrowing. "You mock me, *señor?*"

Jeff licked his lips. He had to play the role of a tough, drifting gunhand . . . but he knew he could push this man only so far.

"I'm trying to get to Vera Cruz," he temporized. "It doesn't matter who I really am."

Vincente said nothing for a moment, then nodded, relaxing slightly. "No, it doesn't," he said softly. He turned slightly and raised his right hand shoulder high and the guns of the four men riding with him were suddenly drawn, trained on Jeff.

"I am sorry," he said to Jeff . . . "but I cannot let you go on. . . ."

"Wait!" Maria moved her cayuse closer to the Mexican leader. "Let father talk to him."

Avilla looked at his niece.

"You know his rules," the girl repeated firmly. "All strangers are brought to him first. He decides."

Vincente sighed.

"Take his gun, Phineas."

Phineas edged toward Jeff, paused as Jeff turned slightly to face him. He had seen what a gun in Jeff's hand could do.

Jeff looked at the Mexican boss of the *Amigos*. "Just so you get one thing straight, Avilla. That girl just saved your life."

He tossed his gun to Phineas who caught it, startled. Vincente smiled. "I think George will be glad to see you," he said.

He swung around to Jack.

"Get him a horse. We're riding."

V

THE *Paseo Grande* ranch spread out along the small and forgotten river, shaded by trees planted more than a hundred years before Father Kingo and his followers. The ruins of an old Spanish presidio looked down from the rocky cliffs beyond, and around a bend in the river was an ancient mission church, its bell tower gone, its walls crumbling.

Until a month ago Father Ortegano rode a mule from Durango to say mass at the church, but now, with trouble flaring all along the northern border, it had become too hazardous to make the journey.

Virtually isolated, big and cattle rich, the ranch had become an armed camp.

The tall man standing at the window of his room was reminded of this as the Mexican sentry paced past his line of vision.

Roger Briscole watched him for a moment, then lifted his gaze past the run of cooling trees to the hot, sterile hills that marked the borders of the savage country beyond the ranch.

Way off in the distance, coming down the old presidio trail, Roger saw riders . . . he turned and picked up a pair of field glasses from a table (a small luxury allowed him) and turned back to the window.

The glasses brought the indistinct figures into focus . . . he could make out Avilla and Maria. He knew the others . . . but the man riding between Avilla and Maria was a stranger. Briscole, though, felt only a sadness for Avilla as he thought: *Another gun for a revolution that would never take place. . . .*

He turned as he heard someone open the door and come into the room behind him. It was a large, airy room in which he was being held prisoner . . . beamed with rough-hewn timbers, the thick adobe walls whitewashed a creamy coolness. Hand-woven Indian tapestries added color to the otherwise meagerly furnished chamber . . . there was a bed, again of heavy timbers, a chest, a mirror and a long trestle table.

The man who came into the room was as tall as Briscole, but better looking and more sure of himself . . . he had passed himself off as the newspaperman at Ansara, but his real name was Cass Borman and he managed this ranch for George Taine.

He strode up to Briscole, a big man in immaculate whipcord trousers and white shirt, the black string tie ends loose, giving him an air of relaxed competence. A good-looking man in his middle thirties (a few years older than Briscole) he wore a clipped military mustache that somehow enhanced his appearance as a manager of American holdings in a foreign land.

"Missed you at dinner," Cass said, smiling.

The newspaperman shrugged. "I'm not very hungry—"

"You look a little poorly," Cass said. He took the field glasses from Briscole. "You need a change . . . a chance to get out of this room." He started to lift the glasses to his eyes.

"Maybe I can arrange a boar hunt. Ever hunt one of these devils? The Mexicans call them *javellinos—*?"

He was studying the far-off riders through the glasses. But he caught Briscole's headshake from the corner of his eye.

Cass lowered the glasses; he put a hand on Roger's shoulder.

"What do you want, Roger?" His tone was friendly. "George said to make sure you were comfortable. You haven't wanted for anything, have you?"

Roger looked him in the eye. "Let me ride out of here, Cass!"

Cass kept his smile, but his eyes were ice blue and ruthlessly direct.

"You know that's impossible."

Roger turned away from him.

Cass studied him for a moment. "It's your own fault, you know. If you'd change your mind about the revolution—"

Briscole's tone was bitter: "What revolution?"

"Avilla's revolution," Cass answered smoothly. "The hope of the poor starving peasants of this country—"

He broke off as Avilla and his group came into sight again down the long, tree-shaded road to the ranch-yard. He placed the field glasses down on the table.

Roger said bitterly: "The peasants will take care of themselves, eventually. I'm sorry for Vincente Avilla."

Cass looked at him, his eyes cold. "Don't be. Vince is getting what he wants out of this."

He turned and left the room. Roger remained by the window, staring out at the hot, desolate hills. . . .

Coming down the tree-shaded road Jeff Corrin could see Texas cattle in the corrals . . . a mixture of long-horn and Hereford and some Brahmas. He also saw armed men all along the way and the feeling came to him that this big ranch was like a fort, self-sufficient and contained and impervious to the troubles around it.

Cass Borman was waiting on the wide and awning-shaded veranda as they rode into the yard. He had an Army holster and Colt belted at his side . . . he came to the head of the steps and smiled at Maria and there was genuine feeling in his eyes.

"Glad to see you back, Maria."

The girl swung down from the saddle like a man . . .
she had a man's way of riding and it was obvious she
had spent much time on a horse. And yet she retained
a soft and feminine aura . . . one never mistook her for
anything but a woman.

She looked up at Cass, not sharing his feelings.

"Where's father?"

"Left for Durango . . . right after you left."

Maria was disappointed.

Avilla had dismounted . . . a Mexican ranch hand was
coming up to take care of the horse.

"On business again, Cass?" Avilla's voice was casual.

Cass nodded. He watched the Mexican leader come up
the veranda steps and pick up the dipper by the big
olla. He swung his gaze back to Jeff who alone remained in saddle.

"Where'd you pick him up, Vince?"

Avilla glanced at Jeff. "Escondido Valley. He was looking for a horse . . ."

Jeff put in, evenly: "All I wanted was a horse, Mister.
I won't bother anybody. I'm headed for Vera Cruz."

Cass looked at Avilla. "Why didn't you give him a
horse and let him go?"

Vincente studied Borman, his eyes lidded. Then: "I
don't believe him."

Cass smiled. "Then I guess there's only one thing to
do. Shoot him!"

Maria was shocked. *"Cass!"*

Avilla shrugged. He dipped into the clay water jug

and drank, like an Apache, just enough to ease the dryness in his mouth.

Cass was looking at the girl, his eyebrows arched slightly. "For all we know he might be a murderer—"

"Even a murderer gets a trial," Maria said sharply. "You can't just—"

"These are troubled times in Mexico," Cass cut in smoothly. "We can't always observe the niceties of the law." He looked at Avilla.

"What do you say, Vince?"

Vince eyed Jeff casually. "He's fast with a gun. That could be good—or bad. Depends on what side he's on—"

Maria cut in: "You promised to let father decide—"

Avilla looked at Cass who shrugged. He motioned to Jeff.

"Get down."

Jeff swung out of saddle. His life was hanging on the whim of these two men, both casual as to their decision. . . .

The ranch hand had gathered up the reins of the horses and was starting to lead them toward the corral . . . Jeff started to move aside, then suddenly whirled, lifted a rifle from one of the saddles, whirled and cocked it in one quick motion.

He leveled the muzzle at Cass.

No one moved.

Surprise and chagrin held the men who had ridden with Jeff and Avilla. Vincente came to stand beside Cass.

He murmured: "See what I mean, Cass?"

Jeff said grimly: "I'll trade you, mister." He was speaking to Cass. "Your life—for a horse."

Cass shook his head.

"You've got five seconds!" Jeff said. He meant it.

Nogales Smith began to ease away, his hand inching toward his gun. Avilla made a slight head motion—Nogales stopped.

Maria said sharply: "Put that gun away, Galahad!"

She walked directly in front of the muzzle, put her hand on it, pushed it aside. "I'll make the trade—"

Jeff tried to push her away . . . Silent Gordon came up behind his head.

Jeff fell against the girl and went down, unconscious. She picked up the rifle as Silent Gordon started to point the muzzle of his gun at the back of Jeff's head.

She looked at Cass. "I saved your life. I want his . . ."

Cass shrugged. "What about it, Vince?"

Vince was looking at Jeff sprawled in front of the steps.

"Maybe we're making a mistake," he said. "But I always like a man who puts up a fight." He turned to Gordon. "Take him over to the bunkhouse. When he's ready to ride, if Mr. Taine isn't back, give him a horse and ride with him as far as the old presidio . . ."

He looked at Maria, his voice softening. "That all right with you, Maria?"

She nodded.

Cass waved to the door. "Come on in. Must be close to a hundred out in that sun . . ."

As Avilla and Maria mounted the steps, Cass glanced toward the men hauling Jeff toward the bunkhouse.

"Galahad?"

He smiled, but his eyes were cold and he would always remember that for a few seconds he had been at the mercy of that unconscious stranger.

VI

NOGALES SMITH squatted by the bunk, his back up against a post and watched as Jeff frowned slightly and reached out with his right hand as if groping for something. He watched with bright-eyed interest, saying nothing until Jeff opened his eyes and turned his head toward him.

The bunkhouse was long and narrow. It had been built barracks-style, with doors at both ends open to catch the breeze. Inside the thick adobe walls it was at least twenty degrees cooler.

Except for Nogales and Jeff the bunkhouse was empty. The runty outlaw said casually: "I was about to give up on you, Galahad."

He held up three fingers. "How many?" He held them close to Jeff's face.

Jeff's pain-filled eyes focused slowly . . . he shifted his gaze to Nogales, who repeated the question.

"Three," he muttered and pushed himself up into a

sitting position and ran his fingers slowly down the bruise on the back of his head.

Nogales grinned. His voice was casual. "Guess you're all right." He straightened. "Feel like eating?"

Jeff ran his tongue across his lips. "Thirsty."

Nogales walked to the big clay jar standing by the door . . . there was a cover over the mouth to keep out insects. He brought Jeff a dipper of lukewarm water.

Jeff drank it all. Nogales hunkered down again, watching. Jeff touched the lump on his head again. He looked at the gunslinger. "Who?" His voice was hard, angry.

"You're lucky to be alive," Nogales said. He walked to the door, looked out toward the gallery. Dishes clattering and men's rough voices drifted back. He turned to Jeff. "You sure you're not hungry?"

Jeff swung his legs over the bunk and stood up and unconsciously dropped his hand to his empty holster. He looked at Nogales, his eyes questioning.

"You'll get your Colt later." Nogales gestured to the gallery. "You better come along, Galahad. They feed well here."

Jeff joined the small man at the door. There was a dull pain at the back of his head and his legs were weak, as though he had been a long time in a sick bed.

He leaned against the door jamb and looked across the big ranchyard . . . the galley was a square building closer to the creek.

He nodded. "I'll give it a try."

They walked the hundred yards to the galley. The *Paseo Grande* ranch, he learned later, had a caste system . . . its hired hands ate in shifts, the Americans first, the Mexican ranch hands last. Perhaps for compensation, but mostly because of tradition, the Mexicans had a longer siesta period.

Besides Silent Gordon, Cob Eaton and Nat Hines, whom Jeff had met, there were at least a dozen other American gunhands. They gave Jeff a cursory glance and went on eating.

Jeff eased onto a long bench beside Nogales. Gordon sat across from him. The ugly *segundo* eyed him briefly.

"You feel up to riding?"

Jeff looked at him.

Gordon said: "Boss said you could go." He waved to the platters of food. "Go ahead and eat." His grin had a cold wickedness rather than warmth. "Be a long time between meals after you leave here."

Nogales was heaping his plate with steak, potatoes, beans, tortillas and everything else he saw on the table. He was, Jeff observed without interest, a small man with a big appetite.

Jeff ate very little. He drank a lot of water.

Gordon finished and rolled himself a cigarette. He watched Jeff for a minute, then: "You through?"

Jeff nodded.

Gordon stood up. "Let's go."

He motioned to Nat Hines who pushed away from the table and joined Silent, the others watching curiously. The three of them went out to the corral.

Jeff said: "What changed the boss' mind?"

"Mr. Borman?" Silent shrugged. "Reckon it was Miss

Taine." He paused at the corral bars. "She's the only one around here can get what she wants from Borman. And her uncle Vince," he added casually.

Jeff frowned. "Miss Taine?" The name had a familiar ring, tantalizing him. Yet he knew he had never seen this girl before.

Gordon nodded. "George Taine's daughter. Taine owns this place—but Cass Borman runs it."

He waved toward a half dozen horses huddled in the shade of an old pepper tree inside the corral.

"Take your pick."

Jeff moved close to the corral bars, studying the grouped animals . . . the name of George Taine now clicked into place. A big man in Texas—friend of the governor, chummy with a state senator, owner of a big ranch just north of Eagle Pass, the Triangle T.

Jeff knew George Taine, having met the rancher at Ranger headquarters once or twice—and George Taine would remember him.

Maria and Vincente Avilla came out of the ranch house to watch. The *Amigos'* boss remained on the veranda, being joined by Borman a few moments later—but Maria joined Jeff at the corral.

Her smile was friendly enough. "How do you feel now, Galahad?"

Jeff shrugged. "Well enough."

"I saved your life," she said casually. "Aren't you going to thank me?"

He looked at her for a long moment and she began

45

to flush. Gordon's eyes narrowed and his hand slid down toward his gun.

"Thanks," Jeff said dryly.

Her voice was cold now. "Gordon and Hines will ride with you until you're clear of the ranch. Vera Cruz is southeast. You'll have to find your own way."

Jeff turned to the ugly *segundo*, extending his right hand. "I'll need my gun. I'm not looking for trouble, but with things the way they are in Mexico it might be hard to avoid it."

Gordon glanced at Maria who nodded. He turned to Nat Hines, lounging against the corral bars.

"Get his gun."

Nat Hines went into the bunkhouse.

Maria said: "You don't like Mexico, do you?" There was a faint resentment in her voice.

Jeff was watching the two men on the veranda . . . his attention drifted to a window of the sprawling ranch house, half shrouded by shrubbery . . . he glimpsed a man standing by the window, inside the house, looking out. . . .

Roger Briscole?

Maria's sharp voice intruded into his speculation: "Do you?"

He put his gaze on her, his voice level: "I didn't come here for my health, Miss Taine."

She nodded. "Father is due back any time." She turned to Gordon. "Maybe we should wait—"

Nat Hines appeared, holding Jeff's sixgun. He handed it to Gordon.

The last thing Jeff wanted was to meet her father. He said harshly: "I don't like being the mouse in a cat-and-mouse game. Am I leaving—or staying?"

Maria looked at Gordon. "Give him his gun."

Gordon handed the weapon to Jeff. "It's empty," he said. "You've got shells in your cartridge belt. Don't reload until you're on your way to Vera Cruz."

Jeff slipped the gun into his holster.

"I'll take the roan," he said, waving toward the horses in the corral. "The one with the left front stocking."

Gordon signaled to a Mexican wrangler hunkered down, smoking, in the thin shadow cast by the barn. The man shuffled over. He was in his fifties—a seamed, leathery-faced man with a slight limp. He looked at Maria for orders, ignoring Gordon and Hines. She told him in Spanish what she wanted; he nodded and went into the barn for a rope.

Maria turned to Jeff. "If you weren't so quarrelsome," she said lightly, "my uncle could use you. But he doesn't trust you—"

"Revolution isn't my line," Jeff cut in.

"What is?" Gordon asked. He looked amused. "Bank holdups? Stagecoaches? Or just plain murder?"

Jeff looked at them, reacting to the amused lightness of their conversation. They were smug; he was just a drifter they were being momentarily kind to.

He turned away toward the corral gate.

Silent reached out, yanked him around.

"When you're asked a question around here, answer it!"

Jeff knocked his hand away. "Go to hell!"

Silent instinctively went for his gun. Jeff drove his fist into Silent's ugly face, knocking him back against the corral bars . . . he stepped in quickly, before the *segundo* could recover and sank his fist into the gunman's stomach.

Silent doubled up and dropped his gun and Jeff stepped on it, then froze as he heard a gun cock behind him.

"Nat, no!"

He turned slowly to Maria's voice . . . she was standing between him and Hines, who had a gun leveled in his hand.

Nat Hines slowly put his gun away.

Maria turned to Jeff, her face blazing. "Next time I'll let them shoot you!"

Jeff said levelly: "I don't take to being shoved around."

Maria shook her head. "With that temper I really don't know how you've managed to live this long."

She turned to Gordon, who was braced against the corral bars, breathing with difficulty—the gunman lifted his finger tips to probe at his cut lip.

"Go lie down in the bunkhouse," Maria suggested. "I'll get someone else to ride with him."

Silent pushed her away . . . he took an unsteady step toward Jeff, his eyes hating. . . .

Avilla's voice stopped him. "Gordon!"

The *Amigos'* boss and Cass Borman were coming toward them. Avilla pointed toward the bunkhouse. "Do as Maria says."

Gordon looked at Jeff. "Some day I'm going to kill you!"

He picked up his gun, jammed it into his holster and walked slowly to the bunkhouse.

Avilla and Borman paused beside Maria. Avilla's gaze was curious, studying Jeff.

Borman's smile was more a sneer. "You're the most untactful man I've ever met. You're just begging to be killed."

Jeff said grimly: "I didn't ask to come here."

Maria intervened, her face flaming. "No, you didn't. And the sooner you leave, the better!"

The Mexican wrangler was at the corral gate with Jeff's roan, saddled and ready.

As Jeff started to mount, Maria said: "Just a moment." As Jeff turned: "He'll cost you one hundred dollars."

Jeff shook his head.

Avilla moved up beside his niece, smiling a little. Borman's eyes were cold. "We're not giving you that horse, Galahad."

Maria said, "You told us at Escondido Valley that you would pay that much for a horse—"

"That was then," Jeff interrupted grimly. He touched the bump at the back of his head. "Way I figger it now, you owe me this horse."

Maria stared at him, shocked at the unmitigated gall of the man. Then she exploded: "Why, you . . . you . . ." she spluttered, at a loss for the proper ladylike words.

Avilla made a quick gesture to the saddled roan. "Go on," he said harshly to Jeff. "Get out of here!"

Jeff swung aboard.

"Just keep riding," the boss of the *Amigos* added grimly. He waved a hand southward.

Jeff reached down for the canteen hanging from his saddle. It felt empty. He shook it to make sure.

Avilla grinned coldly. "*Señor*, for a man such as you, what is water? There are springs out there in the desert . . . somewhere. . . ."

Jeff eyed him. Cass Borman was smiling . . . Maria was too angry to care.

"The desert, *señor*," Avilla said harshly. "Or a bullet. It is your choice."

Jeff studied the three of them for a long hard moment, then he started to swing away.

Borman said: "Ride with him, Nat. See that he gets a good long start for Vera Cruz."

As Hines started for his horse the Mexican wrangler suddenly pointed toward the tree-shaded road.

"El patrone!"

Jeff turned, a chill sluicing through him.

Three riders flanked the fringe-topped buggy that rolled at the head of four canvas-covered wagons. The driver of the buggy was a Mexican. The big fleshy·man on the seat beside him, in wilted white shirt and rumpled town clothes was George Taine.

They swept into the yard, the American armed guard grim-faced, dust-covered. George Taine turned and motioned the wagons to a stop. Then, glancing toward the small group by the corral, he said something to his driver. The buggy swung toward them.

Jeff sat rigid in his saddle.

The buggy pulled up a few feet away. Taine glanced at Jeff, then put his attention on Avilla, Cass and his daughter.

"I've got the guns," he said to Borman. Then, to Avilla. "There's a military contingent coming up out of Mexico City, headed by General Franco. They'll be in Durango in three days . . ."

Avilla nodded, a brightness in his eyes.

Taine started to step down from his buggy. He paused, glanced at Jeff, then looked startled, recognizing the ex-Texas Ranger.

Borman was watching him; he said sharply: "You know this man, George?"

Taine looked steadily into Jeff's cold eyes . . . after a long moment he took a breath, shook his head. "No. For a moment I thought I did—"

Borman pressed him. "You sure?"

Taine swung his attention to Cass; he was a man of hard temper. "Of course. Who is he?"

Avilla answered: "Found him at Escondido Valley. Fast with a gun." He smiled faintly. "A man with a mean temper—he said he was looking for a horse—"

"So *he* said," Borman cut in harshly. "I don't believe him, George. Neither does Vince."

Taine pinned his cold glance on Jeff. "Get down!"

Jeff hesitated, then dismounted.

"What do you call yourself?"

51

"Pete Galahad."

A flicker of amusement went through Taine's eyes. "Give me thirty minutes to get washed and rested. Then come to the ranch house. I want to talk to you."

He started for the house.

Borman said: "He's trouble, George."

Taine looked at him. "We ran into a bit of trouble picking up those guns. We lost Nick. We can use a replacement."

He took his daughter's arm. They went into the ranch house, and Jeff, unnoticed, let out a long, slow breath of puzzled relief.

VII

BORMAN WAITED until Taine and Maria had gone into the ranch house. He slapped his palm gently against his holster, his only outward sign of anger . . . his eyes studied Jeff, narrowed and suspicious.

"You'd be better off heading for Vera Cruz," he suggested. "I'll tell George you didn't want the job."

Jeff was remembering the look in Taine's eyes—the man *had* recognized him. But he had lied to Borman and to Avilla. Why? What did he want?

He shrugged. "I've changed my mind," he said. His voice was casual. "I can always get to Vera Cruz."

The suspicion deepened in Borman's eyes. "You don't

look like the sort of man who changes his mind often," he snapped. Then, pressing: "Get on that horse and get out of here!"

Jeff grinned faintly. Deliberately he drew his empty gun and without haste he reloaded.

Lounging against the corral bars, Nat Hines waited— his glance went from Jeff to Borman. . . .

Avilla waved him off. "I guess he's staying, Nat."

The gunman gave Jeff a slow, hard look, then sauntered off toward the bunkhouse.

One of the Mexican wagon drivers came up. He spoke to Avilla in Spanish. Where did Avilla want the wagons unloaded.

Borman answered, his voice clipped. "Leave the wagons right there! Don't unload them!"

The driver turned and motioned to the others . . . they moved away, toward the Mexican quarters.

Avilla said to Jeff: "If Mr. Taine hires you, you ride with me."

Jeff slipped his loaded gun back into his holster.

"Where?"

"Durango!"

Jeff nodded. He looked at Borman. "The roan's mine?"

Borman said coldly: "We'll talk about it later." He waited, watching Jeff as he turned, went into the bunkhouse.

Then, turning to Avilla, he said harshly: "He's trouble, Vince. You should have killed him right away, when you had the chance."

Avilla said: "We can always kill him." He looked toward the house. "But George is right. We can always use another gun. Especially one like his."

Borman turned to the house. "George knows him, Vince." His voice was flat with conviction. "I wonder why he lied."

Vince shrugged. "Let's take a look at the guns."

The long square boxes were nailed closed and covered with tarpaulin. Borman pried open one of the boxes . . . the rifles were new Winchester repeaters, .30-30. The grease had been wiped from them.

"A hundred of them," Borman said. "And enough ammunition to wipe out an army." He grinned coldly. "There's your revolution, Vince."

Vincente reached down for one of the rifles. His eyes burned with a deep fire. "We'll be ready for General Franco, in Durango. . . ."

Borman put his hand on Avilla's, holding him. "The guns have been checked," he said. "No sense in wasting time and ammunition."

Avilla looked at him. "I do my own checking," he said. "Even if the guns are new."

Borman shrugged. "If you insist—"

He reached into the box, his hand sliding from the Winchester Avilla had been about to pick up to the one next to it. It had a small notch on the polished wood butt. He handed it to the boss of the *Amigos*.

Avilla pried open an ammunition box, scooped up a handful of shells, loaded the Winchester. He walked to the end of the corral, picked out a distant target on a bare slope and fired rapidly. He was pleased at the results.

Borman watched him slide the rifle back into the long box, nail it shut.

"There's plenty of ammunition," he said casually. "But if all your men start checking out their gun—"

"I'm satisfied," Avilla said. "My men will save their ammunition for General Franco . . ."

He looked off toward the distant, desolate hills, his thoughts leaping into the future.

"If we win in Durango, Cass. . . ."

He did not see the look in Cass Borman's eyes . . . and it was well that he didn't. . . .

Jeff Corrin washed leisurely at the stand outside the bunkhouse. . . . he shaved and put on a clean shirt. No one bothered him. Several hard-eyed gunmen came out to look him over . . . they were a clannish group, these Americans, and it would take a while, Jeff thought, before he would be accepted by them.

Silent Gordon avoided him, acting as though Jeff were not here—but Jeff knew he'd have to watch this man. The others were neutral. If George Taine hired him he'd be just another gunslinger hired to do a job.

Thirty minutes later Jeff knocked on the door of the ranch house. Maria answered. She had changed into a house dress, but she was no more womanly because of it.

She eyed him quizzically for a moment, then motioned him inside.

"Father's waiting for you in the study. I'll take you to him."

Jeff followed her across a big living room dominated by a fieldstone fireplace to a carved oak door. Maria opened it and they went in.

George Taine had changed into a white linen suit, which was the way Jeff remembered him—big, important-looking. He was sitting at his desk, a drink at his elbow.

He said firmly: "Leave us, Maria!"

Maria hesitated, then closed the door behind her. Taine waved Jeff to a chair by the desk.

"You're a damned fool!" he said sharply.

Jeff, about to sit down, remained standing. His eyes narrowed.

"Oh, sit down!" the big man snapped. "If I was going to tell Borman and Avilla who you are I'd have told them before."

Jeff settled slowly into his chair.

"Why didn't you?"

The big man ignored the question. "You looking for that *New York World* correspondent, Roger Briscole?"

"Not particularly."

George Taine frowned. "Then why is Jeff Corrin here? The Rangers have no authority in Mexico."

Jeff leaned forward. "Someone killed my brother, Ben. In a border town called Ansara." Taine's slight head nod indicated he knew the place. "Ben was killed while talking to a man who came in to file a story to the

New York World—a man who claimed he was Roger Briscole."

George Taine's hand tightened on his glass. "Cass never said—" He cut himself off, raised the glass to his lips, his eyes hard, judging Jeff.

"Didn't you leave the Rangers? Forced to resign, as I remember?"

Jeff nodded.

"Then you don't care about what goes on here . . . Avilla's revolution . . . or Roger Briscole? You just want the man who killed your brother?"

Jeff leaned forward in his chair. "What is going on here, Mr. Taine? Besides illegal gun-running?"

George's voice was curt. "Nothing that concerns you— or," his eyes turned bitter, "anything you can help with."

He got up and started to pace behind his desk. He looked drawn now, uncertain.

"Who killed Ben?"

The big man stopped by the edge of the desk, looked at Jeff. "I'm afraid you'll have to find out for yourself. I wasn't there."

"Who sent that wire story for Briscole?"

George Taine hesitated, then said bitterly: "There's nothing you can do, Jeff. You're trapped here—like I am . . ." He paused, listening for a moment, then walked quickly to the study window and closed the inside shutters. It was suddenly gloomy in the big room. He stood there a moment, a dark shadow of a man . . . then, turning to Jeff: "It wouldn't do you any good if you knew . . ."

Jeff asked him, "Who's Cass Borman?"

Taine shrugged. "A man I wish I had never met." He walked back to his desk, sat down . . . Jeff's eyes were becoming accustomed to the change in light. He saw Taine settle back in the chair—he looked suddenly old and worried and less important than he had seemed.

"An adventurer," Taine went on slowly . . . "charming when he wants to be . . . a good manager, but a man without . . ." He paused and the bitterness sharpened in his voice. "Look, who am I to talk about Cass Borman? I went in with him with open eyes. It was his idea to take over this place. A good base, he said, for—"

"Stolen cattle?" Jeff said.

"Contraband," Taine answered. "Stolen and illegal goods, bought for a fraction of their value." He leaned forward across the desk. "I'm a big man in Texas, as you know. And my ranch, the Triangle T, ends at the Mexican border. No one checks my wagons when I cross. . . ."

Jeff nodded. "So that's what made you rich?"

"And Cass Borman powerful," Taine answered.

"What about Avilla?"

Taine shrugged. "I married his sister when he was just a wild young man away at school. Avilla is . . . a misguided man. Cass figured we could use his revolution . . . use Avilla and his small band to divert the Mexican authorities who were getting suspicious. If Mexican troops spend their time chasing the *Amigos*, they won't have time to interfere with us."

Jeff walked back to the desk. He studied the big

man for a moment. "You have that correspondent locked up here?"

Taine nodded. "Technically he's a guest . . . he's covering Avilla's revolution."

"But it's Cass Borman who files his stories?"

Taine nodded again.

Jeff put his hands on the desk, leaned toward the big man. "All right, you've got yourself in a jam, Mr. Taine. That's not my concern. And even if it was, I have no authority to do anything about it." He paused, his eyes hard. "I want the man who killed my brother!"

Taine said heavily: "I told you I didn't know anyone was killed at Ansara."

"Who went with Borman?"

Taine pulled away from the anger in Jeff's gaze. "Gordon, Nogales, Eaton . . ." He shrugged. "Any of them could have." He shook his head. "I didn't see Cass leave."

Jeff straightened, his eyes bitter. "You own this ranch, you said—"

"But Cass runs it," Taine interrupted. "You'll have to believe me . . ." He stood up, glanced toward the window. "If I could get back across the border—"

"You just came back from Durango," Jeff reminded him. "Why didn't you just keep going?"

"Four of Cass' men rode with me," Taine answered grimly. "If I had turned north with those guns I would have been shot."

He put his gaze on Jeff. "That's the way it is, Jeff. I'm as much a prisoner here as Roger Briscole."

"How about your daughter?" Jeff said. "She rides—"

"With her uncle Vincente," Taine cut in harshly. "Besides, she doesn't know what I've been doing with Cass —and I don't want her to know. That's what keeps her alive, Jeff—her not knowing . . ."

He walked to the table and poured himself another drink. "She's all for the revolution—" He turned, glass in hand. "I couldn't care less."

"And Avilla?"

"He's got his guns now . . . he'll be marching to Durango." He drank slowly, his eyes hard. "I have a very strong feeling he won't be coming back."

Jeff turned, walked slowly to the door.

Taine said: "Jeff . . ." and when the younger man turned he added softly, "Neither will you." He held up his half empty glass. "Cass holds all the cards. I found that out too late."

Jeff said grimly: "Don't be too sure, Mr. Taine. I'm a hard man to kill." He walked out then. leaving the big man standing in a pall of gloom and depression.

VIII

THE LATE afternoon sun slanted across the trees ringing the ranch and a wind stirred, bringing a mock feeling of relief from the brutal heat of the day.

The Americans dozed on their bunks for the most part. A few, stripped to the waist, played a lackluster game of cards around a table set by the door to catch the breeze.

Silent Gordon came into the bunkhouse. . . . Jeff was by his bunk, watching the card game. The *segundo* paused a moment, eyeing him, then walked over.

"You're riding with us tomorrow, Galahad. That roan you picked out will be your mount—it'll come out of your wages."

Jeff said: "What kind of wages?"

"Same as the rest of us," Gordon said, "two hundred a month." He turned to the others who had paused in what they were doing—they were waiting to hear what Gordon had to say.

"You all heard me," Gordon said. "We're going to Durango." He grinned crookedly. "I expect this time we'll earn our money."

A man with an old face stirred, sat up slowly on his bunk. He had a sinewy, tough body and he kept a skin tight glove on his right hand, eating or sleeping. It could have been an affectation, a bit of showmanship to draw attention to the fact that he was a professional —a man who lived by his gun. In actuality it was to cover burn-scarred fingers.

His hair was red and it was known he had been born somewhere in Texas, near the Brazos river—he was called Brazos Red. No one knew his real name and he never told.

"Whose idea, Silent?"

Gordon didn't answer him right away. He said instead:

"Anybody got any letters to write, write them now." He paused. "Not all of us will be riding back—"

"*Whose idea?*"

Brazos' voice didn't raise, but it carried a hard and arresting emphasis and now Gordon turned to him.

"Mr. Borman," he said. And there was a subtle challenge in his tone which Jeff noticed. These two men, he reflected, didn't get along.

Brazos Red eased back on his bunk. "Long as it's not that goddam Mex's show!" He fished a long thin black cigar from his shirt pocket hanging on a corner of his bunk, stuck it into a corner of his mouth.

"We heard George Franco is coming north with a hundred troopers. We gonna hoorah Durango before he gets there?"

"We're gonna wait for him in Durango," Gordon said, and a cold light flickered in his gaze as he saw the match in Brazos' hand stop short of the cigar.

"*Wait for him?*" Brazos swung his legs over the side of the bunk and stood up.

Gordon nodded.

"Avilla and his men will be ready just outside of town. We help him beat that Mex general and we get a bonus —a thousand dollars apiece. Mister Borman's orders."

Brazos shrugged. "Guess who'll do most of the fighting," he muttered. He lighted up. He didn't have much use for Avilla's brand of revolutionaries.

Jeff turned, started for the door.

Gordon's hard voice bit at him. "Where you going, Galahad?"

Jeff looked at him. "I don't have any letters to write."
He went outside.

Gordon called after him. "Just be around, ready to ride, in the morning." His voice was ugly as he said it.

Jeff paused outside, by the wash stand, to roll himself a cigarette.

Brazos walked out after him, puffing on his cigar. He watched Jeff for a moment, then: "New man . . . you just come in?"

Jeff nodded.

"What'ud you do to Silent?"

Jeff struck a match, lighted his smoke. He didn't say anything and his face revealed nothing.

Brazos grinned coldly. "He doesn't like me, either. He'll kill you, first chance he gets."

"He'll try," Jeff said.

Brazos looked him over slowly. "Well, you talk tough. Like most kids . . ."

He leaned against the bunkhouse wall and brought his gloved right hand slowly up in front of him.

Jeff's eyes followed it, wondering.

"My maw died when I was still sucking milk," Brazos said. His voice was casual, as though Jeff had asked him and he was bored telling it. "There were seven more of us, all older than me—all of us hungry, all of us runny-nosed. My paw picked cotton, chopped wood and made coffins on the side, to feed us. One day he was called in to work on the gin. He was new at it and he got his hand caught in something . . . don't know what. Tore most of his hand off . . .

"The doctor had to cut him free. Did a nice job. Arm healed around a stump of a hand. But Pa never picked cotton again. Fact is—(Brazos was slowly squeezing his gloved hand into a fist, then loosening it again) he never did a lick of work after that."

Jeff cut in with a trace of impatience. "Sounds like a long story. If you don't mind—"

"*Wait!*"

The word was shot at Jeff as from a rifle . . . Jeff, turning away, paused.

Brazos' gun hand flexed again. "I haven't finished." He took his cigar from his mouth, spat out bits of tobacco, clamped his teeth on it again.

"I was there when the doc cut my paw's hand off. Saw the way he worked. Guess that's when I decided I wanted to be like him—a doctor. Paw wasn't so much to me anymore . . . that doc took his place. I followed him around like a dog . . . finally he said when I growed to fifteen I could work with him . . ."

Brazos paused. Jeff waited, somehow compelled to listen, feeling a strange and distorted need in this man to tell his story.

"See this hand?" Brazos said, holding out his gloved fist. "Got it burned one night, trying to save my paw. Lying dead drunk in a stall, he was. Damn fool set fire to himself with an old pipe, and didn't even know it . . ."

He shook his head slowly, his eyes dark with some

deep inner sympathy for himself. "Man can't be a surgeon with a hand like this, can he?" he asked rhetorically. "But . . . take a good look at it, Galahad . . ."

His outstretched hand jerked and disappeared and suddenly there was his gun in it . . . the draw was incredibly fast and Jeff tensed, his stomach muscles tightening under the deadly menace of that leveled gun.

Brazos Red chuckled coldly. "Just don't go getting any ideas about old Brazos here."

He turned abruptly then and strode back into the bunkhouse.

Jeff watched him, eyes still lidded, shocked—his stomach muscles relaxing slowly.

He was turning away when Nogales Smith came outside. The cherubic-faced outlaw grinned.

"Whatsamatter, Galahad? Brazos shake you up?"

Jeff looked at him. "Is he that way all the time?"

Nogales nodded. "Pulls that story an' trick on all the new men." He moved toward Jeff, taking a bite from a chaw of tobacco. "Hell of it is nobody around here is near as fast with a hand gun. Gordon can shoot rings around him with a rifle—but even he doesn't cross Brazos Red."

Jeff looked toward the bunkhouse.

"You been here long?"

"Longer than most," Nogales said. "Brazos was here first—couple of other men, too. Both of them are dead —Nick was killed yesterday—you heard Mr. Taine tell it." He spat juice into the dirt by the washstand. "The pay's good, but the turnover is bad . . ."

Jeff said casually: "Who does the hiring—Taine or Cass Borman?"

Nogales shrugged. "Borman, usually. Least that's the way it was with us—me, Gordon, Cobb and Nat. We were headed for Vera Cruz, too, but stopped over in Durango. Got into a little trouble over a couple of local girls and wound up in the goddam Mexican clink. Cass —Mr. Borman—did some local bribing and got us out. Five minutes later we were working for him."

He looked off toward the bunkhouse, then back to Jeff, his voice lowering. "How much did you get, Galahad?"

Jeff eyed him, frowning.

Nogales wiped a trickle of tobacco juice from his chin with the back of his hand.

"Look, Galahad . . . no one comes across the Mexican border these days for his health."

Jeff considered. It would be to his advantage to keep the myth going that he was on the run from Texas law.

He shrugged. "Near thirty thousand. I didn't make an exact count."

Nogales whistled softly. "No wonder you wanted a horse and a run into Vera Cruz. A man could live out the rest of his life on that anywhere in South America."

"I don't have it with me," Jeff cut in coldly.

"Of course not," Nogales said, grinning. "I never figgered you for a fool." He chewed on his tobacco cud for a moment, thinking . . . this had been in the back of his mind for a while anyway.

"Tell you what, Galahad," he said, his voice conspiratorial, "cut me in for half and I'll help you get it." He shot another glance back to the bunkhouse. "I was getting ready to pull stakes anyway. Pay's good, like I said—but somehow I always end up broke by the end of the month." He mused a moment . . . "Cards, women . . ." he shrugged. "An' this new job coming up—tangling with this Mex general and a hundred troopers ain't like raiding a few border towns. Going into Durango ain't gonna be too healthy—"

"I'll take my chances," Jeff said shortly.

He started to leave.

Nogales said coldly: "Better think about it, Galahad. I know this part of Mexico. And I also know what they're planning—about you."

Jeff swung back to him.

"Who?"

"Borman and Gordon."

Jeff waited; then, impatient, "What are they planning?"

Nogales' grin was that of a man who had hooked his fish. "One third of what you've got hidden out there somewhere?"

Jeff made a show of reluctance.

"Aw, come on, Galahad," Nogales wheedled. "Twenty thousand dollars is still a lot of *dinero* in South America."

Jeff nodded, his eyes grim.

Nogales said: "Is it a deal?"

Jeff's voice was grim: "You better know your way around out there, if we're going to make it to Vera Cruz."

Nogales grinned. "That's my job. You just stay alive, Galahad." He glanced toward the ranch house. "Borman's orders—soon as the fighting starts in Durango, Gordon kills you."

He turned back to Jeff. "We cut out just before, Galahad. I'll have the horses ready. Gordon'll have his hands full with them Mex soldiers . . ."

"Thanks," Jeff said. Then, as Nogales started to leave: "Just one more thing, Smith. Who went down to Ansara with Borman a few days ago?"

Nogales studied him for a beat, then: "Gordon," he said.

IX

THE CANDLE-LIGHTED dining room had been designed in another era when life had been simpler and times less troublesome. The long oak table seated twelve and at one time this had been the usual attendance . . . now four people were clustered at one end, their voices muted.

George Taine sat at the head of the table. Maria and Avilla were on his left—Borman sat on his right.

The Mexican servants moved silently and unobtrusively from the kitchen and back, but none appeared very hungry.

Avilla appeared lost in thought . . . he was thinking of Durango.

Borman toyed with his wine glass. He was watching Taine covertly, studying the big man. The strain between them had been growing for some time now . . . he had known it would happen, and he had prepared for it.

He lifted his glass now, looked at Avilla. "Here's to Durango," he toasted, "and to a new order in Mexico."

Avilla's eyes came up to him, startled.

Maria said impulsively, "To Uncle Vincente," and lifted her glass, her smile bright. "After Durango all of northern Mexico will be behind you."

Avilla shrugged. "But first—Durango." He lifted his glass to his lips, but his eyes were thoughtful and his voice troubled.

Borman smiled coldly. "You seem unsure—"

Avilla looked at him across the table, his eyes dark and faintly bitter. "In a battle no one can be sure."

Borman leaned back in his chair. "This is a hell of a time to have doubts, Vince." His voice hardened. "We got you the guns you wanted—twelve of our men will be fighting with you. We've committed ourselves, Vince—you've got to win in Durango!"

Maria said quickly: "Of course we'll win!" But her gaze went from Avilla to her father, searching for assurance.

Avilla said softly: "Only twelve of your gunfighters, Cass—?"

"Thirteen," Borman answered, glancing at Taine. "You did hire Galahad?"

Taine shrugged. "Why not? We've been hiring his kind for years."

Cass Borman turned back to Avilla. "I'm keeping Brazos Red and a couple of men here. Just in case—"

Avilla's grin was crooked, cold. "I see that you, also, have doubts." He straightened in his chair and took a deep breath. "Perhaps it is normal to have doubts on the eve of battle." He lifted his glass again, his eyes bright. "Well—here's to Durango—and the revolution!"

Taine put his glass down as he saw Roger Briscole appear in the dining room doorway . . . he was facing in that direction and saw him first.

"Glad you changed your mind, Roger," he said and the others turned to look at the *World* correspondent. Taine waved him to a chair beside Borman. "I was beginning to doubt my own hospitality."

Roger walked over and sat in the chair next to Cass, but he did not look at him.

Borman said indifferently: "He's been on somewhat of a hunger strike while you were gone, George."

The newspaper man watched as one of the servants poured wine into his glass.

"Captivity is hardly conducive to good eating," he murmured.

Maria frowned. "I was not aware that you were being held here against your will." She looked questioningly at her father.

Taine shrugged. "Far as I'm concerned Mr. Briscole can leave any time."

"Of course," Borman cut in smoothly, "We couldn't guarantee his safety, once he left the confines of the ranch."

Roger smiled faintly. "You could, if you wanted to."

Maria was disconcerted. "You've been our guest. I was not informed you felt yourself a prisoner, although I understood you are not in sympathy with the revolution." She looked directly at her father.

"When are you going back to the Texas ranch?"

Taine considered a moment before answering. "Soon," he said.

"Mr. Briscole could go with you," Maria suggested.

Taine eyed Borman, a small smile on his lips. "Of course," he said to his daughter.

Borman didn't say anything.

Roger's gaze moved back and forth between the two men. He smiled faintly. "I'll hold you to it, Mr. Taine."

It was dark outside the bunkhouse when Jeff paused by the well which was enclosed by a lattice-framed structure and interlaced by grape vines.

He lounged in the shadows, smoking, thinking of tomorrow, reassessing his course of action. He knew who had killed Ben, and this is what he had come for—nothing more.

In Durango, he would kill Gordon. And then—well, there was nothing back in Texas for him. And Vera Cruz was as good a place as any. . . .

He didn't see Maria until she loomed up . . . he butted out his cigarette and turned to her and she stopped, momentarily startled. Then: "Oh, it's you, Galahad."

Her laughter was soft and pleasant. "I didn't expect anyone here. . . ."

He said quickly, "I'll leave."

"No—stay." She moved up closer and while there was no moon there was enough starlight for him to see her face.

"I'm curious," she said. "Galahad? That isn't your real name, of course."

He shook his head. He didn't particularly like this woman and he didn't want to get involved in a conversation with her.

But she wasn't about to let go.

"Did you kill anyone?"

He nodded.

"Is that why you're wanted by the American law?"

He said coldly, "I reckon that's none of your business, Miss Taine."

She reacted angrily for a moment, then, surprisingly: "You're right, it isn't." She glanced toward the quiet, darkened bunkhouse. "Most of those men in there, hired by my father and Cass, are the same. But, at least they're fighting for a good cause now . . ."

"Whose cause?"

"The people of Mexico!" There was conviction in her voice.

His tone was cynical: "The *Amigos?*"

"My uncle's revolution. My father supports it. First

the provinces of Chihuahua and Sonora—then all of Mexico."

He shook his head. "Raiding small border settlements . . . hit and run . . . killing people that have nothing to do with your revolution . . . who want nothing of anyone but the chance to make a living—"

"That's not true!"

Jeff shrugged. "When was the last time you were back in Texas?"

She was silent then, looking off toward the darkened hills. "I haven't been there."

He eyed her, curious. "You mean you've grown up here without ever wanting to go into Texas . . . to be part of your father's life there?"

"My mother was Mexican," she said slowly. "I went to school in Guadalajara. My mother's relatives are here . . . my uncle Vincente . . ."

"Your father is a big man in Texas." He was frowning, trying to remember what little he knew of George Taine. There had never been any mention of a daughter connected with publicity about him.

Her voice gave her away. "I'm Mexican," she said. "Texas was our land once . . . it was taken away, by force . . ."

She paused. "You're a Texan?"

He nodded.

"You want to go back?"

"Some day."

She looked at him a long moment. "Maybe I will, too. With my father . . . after the revolution. . . ."

X

THE SUN'S first rays bathed the ruins of the old presidio across the river in soft pink light . . . they came stealing down the stratified walls of the mesa, probing with weightless fingers the quiet trees that lined and surrounded the *Paseo Grande* ranch.

In the yard the riders were mounted and ready, waiting for Vincente Avilla. The wagons, loaded with ammunition and rifles, were hitched and ready to roll.

Jeff sat astride the big roan, flanked by Nogales Smith on one side and Gordon on the other. Thirteen hired guns . . . all of them Americans . . . all of them (except Jeff) outlaws.

Jeff glanced along the mounted line . . . hard men, faces closed, emotionless . . . some with cigarettes dangling from tight lips. This was what they had hired on for . . . they didn't give a damn about Avilla's revolution, Jeff thought . . . they were being paid by Cass Borman and they took orders. Fighting General Franco and his troopers was just another gun job. . . .

But sitting there, waiting, Jeff had the uneasy feeling that this thing for which Avilla had waited so long was going to backfire . . . he felt it, like he felt the prickle at the back of his neck.

The *Amigos'* boss came out of the ranch house, dressed

for travel. With him were Maria, Cass, George Taine—and a man Jeff recognized only from description—Roger Briscole.

They paused on the wide veranda. Maria was dressed for riding . . . there was a determined look on her face. Avilla glanced at the waiting men, then back to Taine's daughter.

"I'd rather you didn't come this time, Maria," he said. He looked at Taine. "Make her stay home, George . . ."

Taine smiled faintly as Maria turned to him, a cold look in her eyes. "You want me to put chains on her, Vince?" He looked at Maria then, and there was concern in his voice. "I've never told you what to do, Maria . . . maybe I should have . . ." He took a deep breath. "Don't go to Durango this time—"

She cut him off. "I have friends in Durango—I'll be staying with them."

"This isn't the same," her father said sharply. "General Franco has field guns . . . no one will be safe in Durango."

She shook her head, unaffected by his wishes; she had never been close to her father.

"Even General Franco won't use those guns to kill helpless people in town."

Cass intervened, his voice grim: "Don't be too sure, Maria—"

She turned sharply to him: "I won't even discuss it with you, Cass!"

He reddened slightly, but held his temper. "I'm only thinking of your safety, Maria. For Vince and these

men . . . well, it's their job and your uncle's revolution.
But why risk your neck—"

"It's my revolution, too," she said curtly. "I want to
be in Durango when Uncle Vince raises his banner
over the town square."

There was no keeping her behind and those men on
the veranda knew it. Avilla glanced at George Taine
and said simply: "I'll guard her with my life, George."

Taine looked at his daughter for a long regretful
moment . . . he saw the gulf between them . . . the gap
he had unconsciously let grow and he knew it was too
late for words . . . maybe too late for anything.

He said quietly, "Good luck, Maria," and turned and
went into the house.

Roger Briscole made a sudden decision. "Let me
ride with you, too, Avilla."

Cass' voice was cold. "No."

Roger glanced at him. "Last night you said I could
leave any time I wanted to. Are you backing out now?
Am I really a prisoner here?"

Maria had stopped at the foot of the stairs; she
turned to look at Borman, frowning. "If he wants to,
let him come, Cass."

Cass hesitated. "I guess it's really up to your uncle,
Maria . . . if he wants to be saddled with a foreign
correspondent who isn't exactly favorable—"

Roger cut in quickly, turning to Avilla: "Maybe I
was wrong about you . . . your revolution. Let me go
to Durango and find out."

Avilla shook his head. "You'll be in the way."

Roger appealed to Maria. "I'll stay with Miss Taine."

Avilla considered. If he won he'd need a good press in the United States. This man could give it to him.

He shrugged. "I can't guarantee your safety, Mr. Briscole."

Roger smiled. "I'll take my chances."

Avilla looked at Cass. Borman waved casually. "Good luck, Vince. . . ."

He watched Roger and the girl take their places on the seats of separate wagons. Avilla mounted the horse waiting for him at the tie rail . . . .he glanced back to Borman once and Cass waved again . . . and then they moved out of the yard toward the desolate hills beyond. . . .

There was a wagon road of sorts to Durango from the *Paseo Grande* ranch, but Avilla and his contingent left it at noon, heading south, following an old stream bed in which scoured and whitened rocks reflected the glaring sun. The arid hills moved in on them, rocky and steep-sided, from which chuckwallas and collared lizards watched with beady-eyed interest. . . .

The mounted men were divided into two contingents —half of them, led by Avilla, riding forward of the wagons—the others, with Gordon in the forefront, riding behind.

Jeff rode loose in the saddle, relaxed, his eyes lidded. Almost as soon as they had left the wagon road Gordon had dropped back so that he was riding almost alone behind the rear group of riders . . . and Jeff could feel the killer's eyes on him, alert and watchful.

Gordon was taking no chances that Jeff would slip away. . . .

The ancient dry creek meandered between the hills. Here and there small algae-covered pools of water appeared, close to the banks, protected from the drying blaze of the sun by overhanging mesquite or cholla.

Finally, at a turn in one of the innumerable bends of the *arroyo* a spot of light flashed across Avilla's path. It moved back and forth, a reflection of the sun, man-directed.

Avilla raised his right hand . . . the riders and the wagons behind him halted.

High up on the slope above the creek a man in ant-hill sombrero and crossed bandolier appeared. He waved his rifle in signal to the men below. . . . Avilla waved back.

They rode on now, and ahead of them the river banks grew trees, mostly cottonwoods and some willows, an occasional live oak. And there was water now under the horses and the wagons, shallow but running.

The walls of an old mission church, abandoned, its walls crumbling, came into view . . . then a dozen or so adobe huts. Once, a long time ago, Father Kingo had built this mission and this town, Santa Lucia, one of a string of missions the padre had built in what was then called the *Pimeria Alta.* Now this settlement was forgotten even by those in power in Mexico City. . . .

This was the hideout of Avilla's *Amigos* when they

were not raiding . . . a motley group of men of all ages, bound by a common cause, a hatred of the men in power in Mexico City, and a strong loyalty to Vincente Avilla. Most of them had a price on their head . . . most of them would be promptly hanged if caught by Federal troops.

They had their women here, their children—they lived without a future and only a burning, bitter hope.

A giant of a man, bearded, bare-chested, holding an old single shot Krag rifle came out to meet Avilla. The others, men, women and children straggled behind. He embraced the *Amigos'* boss, lifting him off the ground, while the others looked on.

"You have the guns, Vincente?" he asked, and it was a desperate cry . . . "you have the guns . . . ?"

Avilla broke free of the other's embrace, grinned. "In the wagons, Tomas. Guns for everyone."

Tomas turned, waved to his men. They ran to the wagons, hauled out the rifle boxes and ammunition cases . . . they cried and laughed like children at the shiny new Winchester repeaters, the boxes of shells.

The guns were quickly handed out, the bandoliers filled. Avilla gave orders to Tomas. "There will be no useless firing, Tomas . . . no wasting of ammunition. Tomorrow we ride to Durango."

Tomas nodded. He turned and bellowed Avilla's orders to the men, then turned back to Avilla.

"It is true? We hear that General Franco is marching on Durango . . . ?"

Avilla nodded. "With a hundred troopers—the pride of Mexico City."

Tomas grinned. "And we, Vincente?"

"We'll be there, waiting for him."

Tomas' big hand tightened on the stock of his new Winchester. "The *Americanos*—they will fight?"

Avilla smiled coldly. "They'll be in Durango—with me. They have been promised a bonus—for money, *si*, Tomas, they will fight."

He put a hand on Tomas' powerful shoulder. "You will lead your men. You will be waiting outside of town . . . in the old *arroyo* that cuts south of the Mesa Blanca . . . When General Franco attacks the town you will attack him—from behind."

Tomas rubbed his palm lovingly over his rifle. "I can't wait, Vincente! After all these years . . . that fat pig, Franco . . ."

"He will have a hundred soldiers," Avilla warned. "They are trained to fight. It will not be easy."

Tomas shrugged. "Come . . . you camp here tonight . . . no?"

Avilla nodded. "We leave early in the morning."

Tomas turned and signaled to the women behind him. "We eat well tonight, Vincente."

Then his gaze brushed over the mounted men . . . they were eyeing Tomas and Avilla and the ragged group of revolutionaries, aloof, cold. Tomas sensed their faint contempt and anger made its brief flare in his eyes and then faded.

He turned back to Avilla, smiling, bitter: "A half

dozen of your brother-in-law's steers, Vincente. For tonight's barbecue. He has so many . . . we didn't think he'd mind . . ."

Avilla shrugged.

Walking toward them, Maria said: "No, my father doesn't mind, Tomas."

Tomas looked past Avilla, seeing Maria for the first time now. He swept his hat from his head. "Maria . . . I . . ."

She was smiling. "It is good to see you again, Tomas," she said.

Tomas picked her up, hugged her.

Maria gasped, laughing: "You're crushing my ribs, Tomas . . ."

He put her down, held her at arm's length, glad to see her. Then, soberly: "Why are you here?"

"I'm going to Durango with you," she said.

Tomas glanced at Avilla . . . Avilla shrugged.

Maria said: "Oh, don't look so uncomfortable, Tomas. I won't be in the way." She glanced toward the huts. "I'd like to wash . . . chat with your wife, Felicia. . . ."

She left them.

Tomas looked up at the waiting, mounted men. "Please," he said quietly . . . "make yourselves comfortable. We will eat soon . . . we will celebrate . . ."

XI

THE BIG COOKING fires lighted up the shadows of the old village. The ruined church, its cross and its bell tower gone, seemed to look sadly upon the scene, remembering with what hopes Father Kingo had built it and to what low estate it had now fallen.

A half dozen carcasses of Paseo Grande beef turned slowly on stout pole spits, basted and presided over by the women of the village. Pots of beans simmered on the fire and there was laughter from the men, smiles from the women and happy play from the children.

It was celebration time for the *Amigos* . . . but for many of these rough Mexican peasants, Jeff thought, this could be their last good meal. . . .

Here, as at the *Paseo Grande* ranch, the American gunslingers did not mix with the Mexicans. They lined up before one of the spits and took their portions of beans and beef and went off together—a group apart, faintly contemptuous, arrogantly sure of their superiority.

Jeff, too, felt a distance between himself and these men . . . he was apart from the revolution and whatever these people felt. Whatever social justice they might have on their side, was none of his business.

But he was being forced into doing some rethinking concerning Avilla and these men who waited to ride against General Franco tomorrow. The *Amigos* who had been raiding the Texas border towns and who therefore were generally hated, were not the bandits he had expected. Maybe they had been misled into thinking the raids were necessary—a way of stirring up resentment and interest in their plight—a way, too, of obtaining money and food and· guns, for the Lord knew there was little enough of these in the Mexican villages of Sonora and Chihuahua.

Jeff was hunkered down with his plate of barbecued beef and beans when Nogales joined him. The small man glanced at the Mexicans by the fires and voiced the thought shared by his companions.

"They'll cut ·an' run when General Franco's field guns open up on them . . ."

Jeff shrugged. "Maybe. . . ."

Nogales said: "Hell, I know them. They don't like us, not one goddam bit. But they need us . . ."

He started to hunker down beside Jeff, then thought of something. "Can't eat this stuff without havin' something to drink." He set his plate down beside Jeff. "I'll see what I can steal for us. . . ."

He walked off into the shadows.

Jeff looked toward the fire . . . Maria was helping Tomas' wife serve. He saw Roger Briscole's tall figure loom up and receive his plate . . . the correspondent said something to Maria and she smiled, then shook her head and Briscole turned toward the wagons.

He paused, plate in hand . . . he seemed out of place here, and he was. But his aloofness was not racial, Jeff guessed—he didn't belong with either group of these men and he knew it.

He saw Jeff then, eating alone, and he walked over, hesitating a moment before saying: "Mind if I join you?"

Jeff made a gesture that indicated he didn't care. Roger squatted down beside him, but it was apparent that he was more used to sitting at dinner tables and after a few uncomfortable moments he got up and found an empty ammunition case which he brought back by Jeff and used as a seat.

"I'm Roger Briscole," he said. "I'm a newspaperman, covering this revolution."

Jeff didn't say anything.

Roger picked at his beans, but he was not really interested in eating.

"You look familiar, somehow," he said. "But I'm sure we haven't met . . . or have we?"

Jeff said coldly: "We haven't."

Briscole took the rebuff and was silent for a moment. Then: "What do you think of them?" he asked, indicating Avilla and his *Amigos* with his chin. "Have they got a chance against General Franco?"

"I'm not being paid to think," Jeff answered curtly.

Roger said coldly, "Just to kill . . ." He stood up, knowing he wasn't wanted here. But he took one last look at Jeff. "Sorry if I bothered you. But you do remind me of someone I met before I crossed the border. In Austin, I think . . . Texas Ranger headquarters . . ."

He was talking about Ben, Jeff knew . . . there was a

strong family resemblance. He didn't want this man to pursue it.

"Maybe," he said harshly, "on a wanted poster."

Nogales Smith came up with a bottle and this decided things for Roger—he moved away, toward the wagons.

Nogales hunkered down beside Jeff and set his bottle down on the ammunition case Roger had brought up.

"Pulque," he said. "Made by Mex, tastes like Mex . . . but what the hell, it gives you a solid feeling in the gut a man needs just before a fight."

He looked off toward Roger melting into the shadows. "What'ud he want?"

"Company, I guess," Jeff answered. He shook his head to the pulque bottle offered by Nogales.

The runty outlaw took a long swig, wiped his lips. His voice lowered. "We'll cut out tomorrow—soon as we can. I've got two good pack animals picked out, a couple of extra canteens. We'll need them to cross the desert . . ."

Jeff was barely listening . . . he was watching Maria by the fire, remembering last night. She did not know what she was getting into . . .

Nogales' voice cut into his thoughts.

"How much time you figger we'll need to get to where you cached the money? Two days? Three?"

"From Durango?"

Nogales nodded.

"Two days at most," Jeff said.

Nogales chuckled. "We'll fool them." He glanced toward Gordon, who was with the rest of his men. "Gordon will figger we'll head for Vera Cruz, or Tampico. But we'll go west instead, Galahad. There's a small fishing village on the west coast of Mexico—a place called Guaymas—"

He paused as one of the longriders came by. Nat Hines paused, looked down at Nogales, said: "Where'ud you hijack the bottle of pulque, Smith?"

Nogales pointed. "Church. They got a mess of them stacked up in the old wine cellar."

Nat Hines looked back toward his group. "Hey!" he said loudly. "I've found out where they keep the booze!"

Several men joined him—they moved off quickly toward the church.

Jeff let his gaze wander to Briscole, standing alone by one of the wagons.

"That correspondent," he said, "how does he get his stories back to his paper?"

Nogales grinned. "Cass Borman does it for him."

"Borman?"

Nogales wiped his gravy-stained mouth with the back of his hand. "Sure. Gordon goes along, just to make sure nothing goes wrong."

Jeff was silent a moment, trying to pin down a discontent within him. Ben had been killed trying to find out what happened to the *New York World* correspondent.

He glanced toward Roger Briscole, a shadow by the wagon. Damn it, Jeff thought, I don't owe that man anything. But he owed his brother more than just getting his killer—he owed Ben what Ben had started out to do.

Find out who was behind the *Amigos*.

And that man was Cass Borman!

XII

GEORGE TAINE looked out his window at the night and he realized how Roger Briscole must have felt as one of Cass' men paused outside to light a cigarette.

Brazos Red was not overt in his watch of Taine's bedroom, but his presence was nonetheless real and Taine knew full well he was now a prisoner in his own house.

He picked up the brandy decanter and poured himself a drink and as he sipped it he reviewed his mistakes . . . the most bitter being his tieing up with Cass Borman.

George Taine did not excuse himself . . . he saw himself clearly for what he was . . . an opportunist, a man who had grabbed at money which meant power in any language and in any country.

He had thought he could handle Borman and outfox him . . . he was the one who had eventually been outfoxed.

He had married Maria's mother for the ranch she

owned here, not for love, although he had been tender to her and never mean. When Maria came along he had been glad to send her off to school . . . by then he had seen, with the help of Borman, a way to make his small holdings in Texas grow through contraband and stolen cattle . . . looting the small ranches on both sides of the border.

He was a big man now. He claimed dinner invitations at the governor's mansion . . . he was an honorary Captain in the Texas Rangers . . . and he had nothing.

He finished his drink and turned at the knock on his door, expecting it, wondering why it had taken Cass so long to come to him.

Borman walked slowly to the table by the window and poured himself a drink. He turned and looked at Taine and held up his glass:

"Here's to Vince's revolution, George."

Taine kept his glass in his hand, turning it slowly between his fingers.

"He's not going to make it, is he, Cass?"

Borman shrugged.

"I thought you were in love with my daughter." Taine's voice was bitter.

"I am," Cass replied. His voice was casual, his eyes studying Taine.

"Love—or want?" Taine said. "There is a difference, Cass."

Borman smiled. "Not to me."

Taine saw Brazos Red outside the window . . . a chill

went through him. But the gunman took a long drag on his cigarette, then moved away.

"You let her go to Durango," Taine said. "If you loved her you would have stopped her."

"That was your job," Cass said. He took a long sip of his brandy, then looked at Taine, considering something.

He smiled. "Tell me, George—how much is Maria worth to you?"

Taine searched Borman's face, trying to find a clue to the man's thoughts.

"I've got a half interest in this place—and in the Triangle T. But we've never put anything down on paper, have we, George?"

He looked down at his brandy glass, slowly sloshed the liquid around.

"Something happen to you, George, and I'm left out in the cold . . ."

Taine felt the chill reach down his spine.

"Let's put it this way," Cass continued. "Your daughter is in trouble. She's in Durango with Avilla, and General Franco won't give her any special favors. If she isn't shot, she'll get twenty years in prison, at least. And you know what a Mexican prison is like—"

Taine said harshly: "If Franco wins!"

Cass turned and set his glass down on the table. "He'll win."

Taine took a deep breath to smother the sinking feeling inside him. "You made sure?"

Cass nodded. "Every move." His smile was serene,

confident. "I got Vince his guns. *You* picked them up for him . . . that way he trusts you . . . and if something goes wrong he'll blame you—"

"Something will go wrong, of course!"

Borman laughed. "Of course. Only one out of every five of those new Winchesters will fire. And the ammunition—" His shrug told it all.

Taine looked at him, contempt in his eyes. "Why, Cass? That's what I want to know—*why?*"

"*We* used him!" Borman snapped. "You were in it with me, all the way!"

It was the truth, and George Taine turned away, his face crumbling.

"All right," he whispered. "I knew Vince never had a chance. But . . . this way. . . ."

He turned and looked bitterly at Cass. "It's mass murder!"

Borman shrugged. "We can't hold onto this ranch much longer, George. The Mexican government knows we're implicated . . . sooner or later Federal troops will move in on us."

"What do you want?"

"Your signature on a paper," Cass replied. "Giving me only what is mine anyway. A partnership in the Triangle T ranch."

Taine considered. It was true . . . the time had come to pull up stakes in Mexico, move back across the border. There no longer was need for this place . . . no need for further risk of running contraband. The Triangle T was big enough and he had enough money.

He nodded. "What about Maria?"

"I'll take some men to Durango," Cass said, "and get her out before the fighting starts."

George studied Borman, knowing he had to trust this man—he had no other choice.

"We've worked together a long time," he muttered. "About Maria—that's a promise, Cass?"

Borman said: "It's a promise."

George walked to his desk and sat down, taking out paper and pen . . . he wrote quickly, then dried the paper, handed it up to Borman.

Cass read it, nodded, then: "One thing, George. Date it two years back." His smile was cold. "I don't want it to appear like a last minute deal."

Taine shrugged. He dated it the way Cass wanted it and Borman added his signature to the agreement.

He said: "This satisfies me, George."

He went to the small table by the window, glanced out. Brazos Red was in the shadows, smoking. Cass nodded his head slightly, turned as George came up.

"Let's drink on it," he said. "To a new deal for both of us in Texas."

He handed George his glass, picked up his own. He raised it to the level of his eyes.

George said: "To a new deal—"

The shot came through the window glass, tearing into Taine's chest, just below his upraised arm. The big man staggered, dropped his glass . . . he turned and saw Brazos Red just outside the window, a gun in his hand and then his glazing eyes went to Borman and he knew in that brief moment before death that Cass had won it all. . . .

The Mexican servants were clustered around Borman as he knelt by Taine's body. They looked on dispassionately; they were not involved.

Nor were the hired Mexican hands who worked the ranch. They had a loyalty to Maria, but she had gone with Avilla. And none of them cared to cross Cass Borman.

Cass pointed to the shattered glass. "The shot came from outside. There is a traitor among you . . . I will see that he is hanged!"

The servants listened stolidly, not believing, but doing nothing. They placed Taine's body on his bed and left.

Cass went to Taine's desk, folded the partnership agreement and tucked it into his coat pocket. There were several places where he could get the paper witnessed and notarized before he showed up at the Triangle T in Texas with a sad tale of a revolution that went wrong and the unfortunate death of his partner, George Taine.

Brazos Red and two other hard-eyed Texas gunslingers were waiting for him outside. They were mounted . . . Brazos held the reins of Borman's horse.

"We're going to Durango!" Cass said. And then, smiling: "Something I promised George Taine!"

No one made a move to stop them as they swung away from the ranch house, rode off into the night.

XIII

DURANGO sprawled on a windswept, dusty plain, baking under the afternoon sun. Goats ran untethered through the alleys and *calles* of the town, as did various species of chickens, some of them as wild as desert grouse.

The town lay astride the main road north out of Mexico City and it was a center of commerce for most of the high desert area. No other settlement of consequence lay within a hundred miles . . . whoever held it would control most of Chihuahua and Sonora.

The local *jefe*, Camillo, met Avilla and his party in the plaza . . . he came forward mopping his forehead with a red bandanna, a fleshy, middle-aged man in rumpled clothes. He knew who Avilla was, and why he was here, but he was powerless to do anything about it.

The mounted *Americanos* with Avilla made sure of this. He glanced at the wagons and smiled at Maria, but his heart wasn't in it.

"Quarters for these men," Avilla directed. "A place for my niece, Maria."

Camillo nodded vigorously. "Of course . . . of course . . ." He gestured to one of several men lounging in front of a cantina. "Fetch Paola . . ."

The man disappeared inside and Camillo turned back to Avilla.

"You are staying in Durango—?"

"Until General Franco arrives," Avilla said.

Camillo swallowed hard. "The *Generale* has already made arrangements by courier . . . his men are to be quartered—"

"We are here first!" Avilla cut him off. He was smiling, but his eyes were hard and Camillo nodded again.

"Of course. This way . . ." He pointed. "The *Cantina Delgado* for your men. My humble home, Vincente . . . if you will honor me . . . for you and Maria. . . ."

Avilla nodded, turned to Roger Briscole. "He is an American newspaperman," he said. "He will stay with us . . ."

The mounted column coming up out of the garrison just outside of Mexico City moved steadily, watched along the road by silent old men and children. The detachment had three French artillery pieces and the mounted troopers were among the best of the Mexican Army.

The man who led them was beefy, in his early forties, not much inclined to pomp and social activities. He was a career Army man who had studied military science in France and Spain and, later, in Prussia.

There was unrest in Mexico, General Franco knew, but it had not seriously involved any of his troopers; their loyalty could be depended on.

He had only contempt for the ragged revolutionaries he would face in Chihuahua.

He did not expect a long campaign.

Maria stood on the veranda of Camillo's house, looking across the walled garden to the low hills through which General Franco would come.

Avilla was with her.

He said quietly: "I wish you hadn't come, Maria."

She turned to him. "I have been with you since I left school—I couldn't stay behind now!"

He sighed. "That American, Cass Borman. Are you in love with him?"

She frowned. "I am in love with no one."

He nodded. "I am glad." He looked off. "He would not make you happy, Maria."

She shrugged.

"There is no one . . . no man . . . ?"

She looked at her uncle directly. "The revolution has been my only concern."

He shook his head. "It is not enough, Maria." His voice was gentle. "For some men, yes . . . but for a woman . . ." He shook his head again. "A woman does not fall in love with a revolution."

"There will be time," she answered diffidently, "after General Franco is beaten."

He looked off toward the hills again, pondering. "I don't know," he said slowly. "We have made mistakes . . . we are not liked everywhere." He glanced back to the house. "That American newspaperman in there . . . he called us bandits . . ."

She blazed: "What does he know? Has he seen the

suffering . . . the poverty of the people . . . the arrogance of those in power . . . ?"

He smiled and touched her cheek with the back of his hand. "Perhaps it should be you to lead us, Maria." His hand dropped. "Lately I've had a feeling . . . a bad feeling . . ."

"We have the guns!" she said intensely. "That is enough!"

He looked up at the sun, nodded. "Tomas and the others should be in position now. General Franco will march straight to Durango . . . he will not be expecting trouble here . . . all around us is an open plain. I know what he will be thinking—a ragged bunch of peasants, badly trained, armed with inferior weapons . . . he is thinking he will have to chase us into the hills . . ."

He stood for a long moment occupied with his thoughts, then he turned to her. "Stay in the house, Maria. I will go see how the Americans are doing."

Roger Briscole came out of the house and stopped beside Maria as Avilla left.

He was silent for a moment, then he said quietly: "I hope he wins, Maria."

She glanced quickly at him.

He smiled at the look in her eyes. "But I'll never get to write the story, will I?"

She said angrily: "Why not?"

"You don't know?" He was surprised.

"You've never believed in Uncle Vince's revolution, that's what I know. To you we're just bandits—"

He cut her off. "Not you, Maria." He looked off, the way Avilla had gone. "Not Vincente Avilla, either. Or those men last night, in that village . . ." He paused. "At first that's what I did think. The *Amigos*," he smiled faintly, "do not have a good reputation along the Texas border."

She said: "You'll write your story, Roger. By tomorrow morning, after General Franco is defeated—"

He shook his head. "Either way, win or lose, I won't be leaving here alive, Maria. Your father and Cass Borman will have seen to that."

"My father!"

He nodded. "I was a prisoner at your father's ranch," he said. "There was always a guard at my window. And Borman told me bluntly I'd be shot if I tried to leave."

She couldn't believe it. "Why?"

"Because I found out too much," he said. "I found out your father and Borman were using the revolution as an excuse to keep attention from their running of contraband across the border into the Triangle T."

He looked off toward the distant hills. "Neither Borman nor your father really care about what happens here today. They've used Avilla . . . now they're through with him . . ."

She backed away from him, not believing what he was saying—not wanting to believe.

"No!" she cried. "It's a lie—"

"Why should I lie?" he cut in bitterly. "What have I to gain?"

97

"How—how could you know?"

"It's my job to know—to find out the truth." He smiled, but it was at himself, as he said: "I have an unlimited expense account . . . and you'd be surprised at what money, in the right places, can bring out. Even at your father's *Paseo Grande* ranch—"

"It's not true," she said harshly. "If you were a prisoner, as you say, surely someone back in the United States, your newspaper—"

"Is not yet alarmed," he cut in. "Cass Borman has seen to that. He's been sending back stories, from a small border town called Ansara, in my name."

She stared at him, stricken. "No," she said, but her voice was a weak protest. "Borman, maybe. But my father wouldn't—"

Roger cut in gently: "I'm sorry I won't be able to prove any of this to you, Maria. But I've got a feeling that Borman has arranged it so that neither you nor I will be leaving Durango—"

He turned to go back into the house, but stopped abruptly, fear flaming across his face, as he saw the tall man in the doorway.

Cass Borman chuckled coldly. "Strange, isn't it, the things a man hears about himself behind his back?"

He made a motion and Brazos Red moved swiftly toward Roger . . . the correspondent turned and tried to run. Brazos drew his Colt and fired almost casually.

Roger Briscole was halfway across the yard, toward

the gate . . . the bullet sent him stumbling forward, on his face.

Borman looked at the white-faced girl. "You didn't really believe a word of what he said, did you, Maria?"

She backed away from him, a shocked numbness in her eyes.

"Cass," she whispered . . . "why?" She turned to look at Roger, lying still where he had fallen. "Oh, God, why?"

"You wouldn't want him getting back to the United States with the wrong kind of story, now would you, Maria?"

She stared at him, wondering what was behind that small smile, feeling revolted at the casualness with which Roger Briscole had been shot.

"You—didn't have to kill him," she said. She was moving back, getting ready to run.

Cass moved his head slightly to Brazos Red and the redheaded gunman moved in behind her, blocking her off.

Cass said quietly, "You're not afraid of me, are you, Maria?"

"I never was," she said bitterly, "until now." She looked past him, to the door. "Did father come with you? Or was Roger right about him, too—?"

"Your father is dead," Cass said bluntly.

She stared at him, a horror in her eyes.

"Oh, come on now, Maria," he said harshly. "He never meant much to you. It was your uncle Vince and his two-bit revolution you cared about."

"You—killed him?"

He shrugged. "Doesn't matter who killed him, Maria." He smiled coldly. "But I promised I'd take you out of Durango before General Franco got here."

"No," she said harshly. "I'm not leaving Durango—"

Brazos Red moved quickly at Cass' nod . . . he came up behind Maria and when she started to scream he clapped a hand over her mouth.

She fought wildly, with greater strength than Brazos had imagined—she almost got free of him before Borman, coming up, struck her across the face with the back of his hand.

She sagged then, staring at him with pained eyes, hating him.

Gabe Beaver, one of the two other men with Borman and Brazos came to the door behind Cass. He said, "The horses are ready, Mr. Borman."

Borman glanced at him, nodded. He turned back to Maria, his voice cold now, definite.

"I'm saving your life," he said. "Some day you'll thank me for it."

Brazos said: "What about the others, Mr. Borman? Gordon, Nogales, Cobb Eaton and—"

"They're being paid to fight," Borman said grimly. He looked off, toward the hills. "This time they'll earn their pay!"

XIV

THE AMERICANS had taken over the *Cantina Delgado,* Avilla noticed when he entered . . . they were scattered around the tables, most of them killing time with cards, a few going over their guns. They were a quiet group . . . professionals, they were being paid to fight. They would celebrate later—after the fighting was over.

The *cantina* girls had departed, taking refuge with friends in other parts of town. Many of the more frightened townspeople had fled into the hills. Only Paola, a rotund, usually jovial man remained behind the bar in the *cantina,* keeping an uneasy eye on these hard-faced mercenaries.

The boss of the *Amigos* put his quick, restless glance on the man he knew as Galahad, standing alone at the bar, a beer at his elbow. This man disturbed Avilla . . . he couldn't quite put his finger on what it was, but he knew the quick-tempered man did not belong with these others.

Gordon was seated at a table, playing poker with Nogales Smith, Cobb Eaton and Nat Hines. They had come into Mexico together and they usually kept together.

The ugly-faced *segundo* turned as Avilla came into the *cantina.* Like most Texans Gordon was inclined to think little of the fighting prowess of Mexicans, but he had a lot of respect for this man.

He said: "How much longer, Vince?"

Avilla glanced around the room. "Latest word I receieved they were less than two hours' march away."

One of the men at another table, a tough blond kid named Jaster, said arrogantly: "About time."

Avilla nodded. "They should be showing up here just before sundown." He paused, studying these cold-eyed men, knowing how much he depended on them.

"I'll be joining my men just outside of town. Gordon will be in charge here . . ."

He looked over that silent, waiting group—no one raised any objections to this. But he noticed a cool cynicism in the eyes of many.

"I know," he said slowly, "that none of you is here because of a love for me, or Mexico. You are here because you are being paid well. So, I will appeal to what is important to you. If you fight well, in addition to the bonus Cass Borman has promised you, I will personally see that you are handsomely paid. If we lose—" he shrugged, his face grim, "well, General Franco will attend to that—"

Jaster said contemptuously: "Don't worry about us. We'll do the fighting. You just keep your men out of our line of fire—"

Avilla turned, studied the cocky young gunman for a moment, holding back the rise of his anger.

Gordon said, hard: "Shut up, Jaster!"

THE DEADLY AMIGOS

Jaster gave him a look; he was just wild enough to challenge Gordon if he was pushed.

Avilla cut in: "Franco won't be expecting trouble here—not at this time. His men will be tired from the long march—he's expecting to put them up in Durango." He paused. "Your job will be to stop them outside of town."

Gordon frowned. "What about those field guns he's got, Vince?"

"This is an open town," Avilla replied. "General Franco will think twice before using them on helpless people."

"And what will you be doing?" Jaster sneered.

Avilla looked at him. "We'll hit them from the rear—"

Jaster laughed contemptuously. "Figgers. That's about the safest place to be, ain't it? Behind the enemy—?"

Avilla moved swiftly, reaching Jaster before the gunman had time to get up. He backhanded him across the face, spilling him backward. He waited as Jaster, humiliated and raging mad, lunged to his feet and clawed for his gun.

Avilla drew and cocked his gun, beating Jaster by a mile . . . he came within a hair-trigger's breadth of killing him.

Gordon's quick voice stopped him: "Vince! He's just a damn fool kid!"

Jaster's hand moved away from his gun; he stared at Avilla, a thin fear in his eyes.

Slowly Avilla said: "Sit down!"

Jaster straightened his chair, sat down.

Gordon said harshly: "If he makes another damn fool move like that, Vince, *I'll* kill him!"

Avilla let out a tight, angry breath; he nodded. "You just hold them, Gordon. My men will do the rest of the fighting."

Gordon nodded: "We'll hold them!"

He waited until Avilla had left, then he put his gaze on every man in that room.

"We signed on to fight for Vince. And we're gonna hold this town, if it takes every last man of us!"

Gordon settled back in his chair and picked up his cards. "Come on," he growled to Nat Hines, who was dealing. "We got about an hour left. I want to win back the seventy bucks I lost."

At the bar Jeff was growing impatient. He couldn't make a move against Gordon in this room, and he had decided to take Roger Briscole with him when he left. This was part of the job his brother Ben had started—

He caught Nogales' eyes and frowned and Nogales nodded slightly. It was time to go.

Cobb Eaton chuckled as he laid down three aces. He looked across the table to Nogales.

Nogales said: "That beats me, Cobb," and tossed his hand into the discards.

He started to get up.

Gordon said coldly: "Where you going?"

Nogales shrugged. "Outside." He banged his knuckles gently against his chest. "Damn cigar smoke in here is getting to me."

"Sit down," Gordon said.

Cobb grinned. "Yeah—keep playing, Nogales." He checked a piece of paper on which he had been making notations. "Way I got it figgered you owe me one hundred and sixty three pesos—American."

"Take it out of my bonus," Nogales said casually. He looked at Gordon. "I've had enough, Silent. I'm going out for a few minutes . . ."

A small suspicion glinted in Gordon's eyes. He nodded, looked across the room to Jeff.

"Join us, Galahad?"

Jeff said: "I don't play poker."

Gordon made a command motion with his thumb. "Join us anyway!"

Jeff stiffened. The man was pushing him and he saw Nogales lick his lips and shake his head slightly.

Nogales intervened. "Aw, come on, Galahad—take my place for a while. Maybe you'll have better luck."

Jeff shrugged. He watched Nogales go out the back door, then crossed to Gordon's table and sat down in Nogales' chair.

Gordon said idly: "You an' that runt Nogales have been pretty thick, lately. . . ."

Jeff eyed him. Nat Hines was dealing again. Jeff let his cards lay in front of him.

Gordon picked up his hand. He studied them, his voice casual. "You're pretty good with a hand gun, Galahad. We'll find out how good you are with a rifle, when that Mex Army shows up."

Jeff shrugged. "I'll earn my pay," he said. He pushed

his cards away. "I said I didn't play." He started to get up.

Gordon's right hand came up with his Colt . . . he rested his hand on the table, the muzzle pointed at Jeff.

"Cigar smoke getting to you, too?"

Jeff's lips tightened.

Gordon kept his bright blue gaze on Jeff. Aside he said to Cobb Eaton: "Keep an eye on him. I'm gonna check on Nogales."

Cobb drew his gun . . . the others in the room watched with varying degrees of indifference. This was an intramural quarrel, they felt, and they had no stake in it.

Jeff watched Gordon get up and walk quickly across the room to exit through the rear door.

Cobb Eaton said dryly: "Pick up your cards, Galahad. If you don't know how to play, we'll teach you!"

His voice was casual, but the gun in his hand was steady, and it was pointed at Jeff's chest.

XV

Nogales Smith worked quickly, saddling his horse and Jeff's big roan which were stabled with the others in the long adobe structure behind Delgado's *cantina*. At the last moment he had gone into the stable's corral to pick out two pack mules . . . he didn't mind stealing from the Mexicans, but he had a streak of loyalty where it concerned the men he had been working with.

Now he was fastening the first of two big water canteens to one of the pack animals. It would take all the water they could carry, he was thinking, to get them across the Sonoran deserts.

He paused as he heard a man's step behind him and, thinking it was Galahad, he said: "Glad you could get away—"

He was turning his head as he said this; he stopped, his voice cutting off in a sharp gasp as he saw Gordon lounging against the door framing.

There was a gun in Gordon's hand, and it was held, casually but very directly, at Nogales.

Gordon said, humorlessly: "Cigar smoke was too much for you, eh?" He sniffed the ammonia-pungent air of the stable. "Doesn't smell a whole lot better in here, Nogales."

The small outlaw shrugged; he said nervously: "Hell, I just came in to check the horses—"

Gordon cut him off, his voice cold: "*Two* horses—yours and Galahad's!" He glanced at the pack mules. "And I see you picked out a couple of pack animals, too." His chuckle sent a chill down Nogales' back—he knew this man too well.

"Who were you expecting?"

Nogales said: "Nobody—" and checked himself as Gordon started to walk toward him.

He said in a low, desperate voice: "Cripes, Gordon —don't you believe me?"

Gordon shook his head. He cocked the hammer of his .45 Colt back as he walked and Nogales backed away from him . . . the small man kept backing up until he felt the hard press of stall boards stop him.

Gordon said: "I don't believe you one bit, Nogales. I figger you're planning to run out on me."

He stopped by one of the pack mules, hefted the canteen hanging from the saddle. "Water, too." His cold and deadly gaze fastened on the small man. "Who was going with you, Nogales?"

Nogales eyed the cocked gun in Gordon's hand. He knew lying would get him nowhere with this man.

"Galahad," he said.

"Two pack animals and water," Gordon reflected grimly. "Which way were you headed?"

Nogales licked his dry lips. "I won't lie to you, Gordon. We planned to leave, right after the fighting." This was a small lie and he figured he could get away with it. "Galahad said he'd split with me—"

"Split what?"

"Money he stole—stage holdup out of El Paso, I think. He's got it hid out there, somewhere just north of where we picked him up in Escondido Valley."

"Just you and Galahad, eh?" Gordon's voice was low, chiding—he was the kind of man who pulled wings off butterflies.

Nogales said, without thinking: "I was planning to cut you in on it, Gordon—"

He cringed as he saw Gordon's thumb move back on the hammer. "All right," he said desperately, "I was going it alone with Galahad. I didn't figger you'd miss me—"

Gordon reached out and slapped him across the face with the gun. The metal split Nogales' cheek; he fell against the stall boards and went to his knees.

"Goes to show," Gordon said contemptuously, "you ride with a man for better than seven years an' you never really get to know him."

Nogales pushed himself up to his feet. "You, Cobb, Nat an' me," he said thickly. "We've been close. But I'm older than all of you—not many more days living off my gun for me—"

He took out his handkerchief and held it to the blood coming from the cut on his cheek.

"Ten thousand dollars, Galahad said—my share. Enough for an old man like me. . . ."

Gordon said: "Well, maybe you're right, Nogales." He was thinking he had found a way to kill Galahad, as he had been instructed, without arousing the other men . . . they were adventurers, gunmen who fought for anyone who would hire them—but they had their own code of ethics. They wouldn't stand for anyone shooting another man in the back.

He lowered his gun. "I don't like the setup here, either." He made a motion toward the unseen hills. "And I've got a feeling Vince isn't going to make it." He scowled. "And you know what'll happen to us, if that Mex general wins. A firing squad!"

Nogales eyed him, relieved but not quite sure which way Gordon was leaning.

Gordon said: "Get Galahad out here. I'm riding with you."

Nogales licked his lips. "I don't think Galahad will—"

"He'll cut me in, too," Gordon cut him off, his voice harsh, "or neither one of you will leave here alive!"

Nogales hesitated, a sinking feeling in his stomach. That was one of the curses of riding with a man a long time—you got to know when he was lying. And Gordon was lying now. Gordon was not the kind of man who'd settle for a third of thirty thousand dollars when he could get it all. Nor was he the sort to forget an insult or a humiliation. Gordon had a mean streak a mile long—Nogales knew he hated Galahad for what Galahad had done to him back at the Paseo Grande. And he knew, too, that Gordon would not forget what Nogales had been about to do—

Gordon lifted his gun again. "Get him out here, Nogales!"

Nogales nodded, knowing he had no choice.

"Stand in the doorway and call him," Gordon directed. "I'll be right here, looking down your back!"

Jeff picked up his cards and glanced at them . . . he had been playing without much interest, but strangely enough, his luck had been running wild. He had already won the last three hands and he saw now that he was holding a full house—kings and tens.

Cobb Eaton had placed his gun on the table in front

of him . . . he was studying his cards, holding them close to his vest. Cobb took his poker seriously.

Nat pulled out his pocket watch. "Getting close to that time," he said. He looked at Cobb. "Wonder what's keeping Gordon—?"

He was facing the back door and he saw Nogales open it and stand there, looking in.

Nat said: "Well, Nogales is back, anyway—"

Jeff turned and glanced at the small outlaw. Nogales was still holding his handkerchief to his cheek.

Nogales said: "Galahad, come out here. Something I want to show you—"

Cobb put a hand on his gun. He said to Jeff: "You stay right here." He looked at Nogales. "Where's Gordon?"

"In the stable. He wants to see Galahad. Something about his horse. . . ."

Cobb frowned. "Don't sound like Gordon—"

Nat Hines cut in: "Hell, what do you care, Cobb? If Nogales says he wants Galahad—"

Cobb shifted his glance from Jeff to Nogales for a moment and Jeff's hand snaked across the table, clamping on his gun hand, twisting the muzzle away from him. He lunged erect in the same move, his own Colt coming up, muzzling Cobb.

"If you don't mind," he said grimly.

He twisted the gun from Cobb's hand, slid it to Hines. "I don't want to kill anybody just to quit a poker game," he said. He nodded toward Nogales. "I'll just go see what he wants."

He eased his gun back into his holster and walked to the back door.

Nogales moved back into the alley as Jeff came up—Jeff kicked the back door shut.

He said coldly: "Where's Gordon?" And because he was keyed up, expecting a doublecross, he moved the instant he saw Gordon ease into sight in the doorway of the stable fifty yards up the alley.

Gordon's shot burned across his upper arm . . . he was moving when Gordon fired and he tripped and fell against the *cantina* wall and went down to his knees.

Nogales spun around, knowing he was next . . . he got his gun out and he fired once, hastily, before Gordon's bullets cut him down.

The ugly-faced man came down the alley, his gun smoking . . . he thought he had Jeff and he reacted too late as Jeff rolled aside and fired.

The slugs knocked Gordon back against the adobe wall . . . he was dead as he started to slide down.

Jeff knelt by Nogales' side. The man was dying.

He said: "Sorry, Nogales. Looks like we won't make it to Guaymas . . ."

Nogales sighed. "Guess we won't . . ." His eyes closed. "Aw, hell," he whispered. "Ten thousand dollars . . ."

The *cantina's* back door opened cautiously and Cobb Eaton looked out, a gun in his hand. Jeff's quick shot chipped adobe a foot from his head and he ducked back inside, slamming the door shut.

Jeff turned, ran into the stable. The roan was saddled and ready to go. He vaulted aboard, rode him out, went galloping down the alley. . . .

The hard-faced mercenaries were grouped around Nogales in the alley. Nat Hines knelt beside the older man . . . he glanced at Cobb who was standing by Gordon's body.

"Nogales is still alive," he said.

Cobb walked back to him, looked down at Nogales. The dying man opened his eyes.

Cobb said: "What happened?"

Nogales thought a moment. He was past pain now . . . he felt himself beginning to slip away.

He said, his voice barely above a whisper: "Gordon —went crazy, I guess. Made me call Galahad out—then tried to kill him. Shot me, too . . ."

Cobb said grimly: "Galahad got away?"

Nogales' head rolled. "He's hurt—don't know how bad." His eyes steadied on Cobb's face. "Let him go, Cobb. He . . . he's not one of us, anyway . . ."

Cobb looked back to Gordon's body. Nat Hines said: "Looks like Gordon asked for it, Cobb."

Cobb nodded slowly. He turned and eyed the others. "We got a choice to make. We can cut out—or stay."

Jaster let his hand slide down to his gun. "I told Vince Avilla we'd hold this town. I don't want no damn Mex saying I cut out an' ran from a bunch of greasers, even if they are part of the Mex army!"

This seemed, somehow, the sentiment of all of them. Cobb shrugged.

"Well, General Franco's boys should be showing up any time now. Let's go earn our bonus!"

XVI

ROGER BRISCOLE dragged himself slowly up the steps of Don Camillo's house and paused in the doorway, fighting off a wave of pain and nausea. The bullet had struck him high up in the back and glanced off his shoulder blade . . . he had lain still, playing dead, knowing that any movement would have brought another bullet.

Maria's cut-off scream still lingered in his head—he peered now into the darker reaches of the house, seeing no one.

Don Camillo and his wife had been at home, he knew . . . he called out, his voice cracking with the effort. No one answered him.

I'm going to die, he thought and a twinge of self-pity went through him. Here, in a small Mexican village on a windswept, dusty plain moments before a small and quite insignificant battle for power was to take place.

He had a story to write, but it was not this one— the story he wanted to write was of an American expatriate named Cass Borman and the men he had used—George Taine and Vincente Avilla.

And the men he had left to die here in Durango.

The wave of nausea ebbed and he moved into the house, supporting himself every few steps by leaning against the wall. And then, coming into the big room off the entrance hall he saw why Don Camillo had not answered him.

He closed his eyes, recoiling from the sight—the utter savagery of the scene repelling him. They were dead, both of them—their throats cut.

Cass Borman, he thought, was ruthlessly thorough. Win or lose, Vincente Avilla and his American mercenaries would be blamed for these deaths.

He heard the rider come into the yard and he pushed himself away from the wall, a wild thought ricocheting through his head. *Was it one of Borman's men, come back to make sure he was dead . . . ?*

He tried to run, to find a place to hide . . . he stumbled and fell and lay there, for the moment too weak too rise. . . .

Jeff Corrin came into the house and paused as he saw Roger Briscole lying on the floor of the entrance hall. He had followed a small trail of blood from the garden . . . he drew his gun now as he went to the newspaperman's side, knelt beside him.

Roger looked at him, blinking. Then, relieved: "Galahad . . . thank God . . ."

Jeff cut in grimly: "Where's Maria?"

"Borman," Roger said weakly. He tried to get up, managing to get to one knee. "He came—with some

115

men. Brazos Red . . . shot me. They took Maria away."

"When?"

"About ten . . . fifteen minutes . . ." Roger waved toward the living room. "They killed Camillo . . . his wife . . ."

Jeff considered. He had come for Roger and Maria; he figured he didn't have much time to decide what to do now. He didn't know if Cobb Eaton and the others wouldn't be coming after him—at any rate General Franco would be showing up about now.

It wasn't his fight, he thought . . . it was not what he had come into Mexico for.

He looked at Roger. "How bad are you hurt?"

Roger started to get up, his face twisted with pain. "Right shoulder," he said. "Can't move my arm much . . ."

Jeff ripped his coat off. He saw where Brazos' bullet had gone in and come out . . .

"You're lucky," he said grimly.

He went through the house, found some sheets which he tore into bandages, came back with a bottle of brandy. "Grit your teeth," he said. He poured some of the brandy into the raw bullet holes and Roger gasped, fell back. Jeff put his arm under his head and forced some of the brandy down Roger's throat.

The newspaperman gagged, opened his eyes.

Jeff fastened a rough bandage over the wound, then helped Roger to his feet. "I've got a mule outside," he said. "Think you can ride?"

Roger nodded.

With Jeff's help they went out into the garden. The

116

pack mule was still tied to Jeff's saddle on a lead rope. Jeff helped the wounded man aboard.

"Hang on as long as you can," he instructed. "When it gets too tough, yell out."

Roger said: "Where we going?"

"North," Jeff answered shortly. "I'm taking you back across the border. . . ."

Tomas squatted by his horse, chewing on a desert twig. A hundred men waited with him, armed with shiny new rifles . . . they fingered loaded bandoliers as they waited, their eyes bright, expectant. There was no talking—only the silence of men waiting to go into battle.

Avilla came back to him, field glasses in his hands . . . he stuffed them into his saddle bags.

"The Americans . . . ?" Tomas asked.

"They are ready," Avilla answered.

Tomas grunted. "It will be quick, then." He tossed the twig away. "What shall we do with General Franco?"

Avilla looked off. "What he would do to us—if we lose."

Tomas grinned as he made a swift motion of cutting his throat—

A man came down the line, moving quickly. "They are on time," he said. "If you look, you can see their dust . . . there . . . just below the hill . . ."

Avilla nodded, looked at Tomas. "Just a few minutes more," he said.

Tomas' eyes glittered. "It's the waiting that is hard, Vincente. . . ."

The Americans waited behind the low wall facing the road to Mexico City. Only ten now, rifles ready, eyes slitted—watching the road into the distant hills.

Cobb Eaton, who had taken command of the small group, said: "Hope Vince doesn't take too long . . ."

Jaster spat out the shredded butt of his cigarette. "A hundred Mex troopers, Cobb? Hell, we can hold them off all night, if we have to!"

The Mexican cavalry column moved down the long slant of ground toward Durango. The three French artillery guns rattled along behind. The column moved with the precision of trained soldiers.

As Avilla had predicted, General Franco was not expecting trouble. But he was a military man, and a good one—and he was never careless.

He moved up along the column, the stub of a short, black cigar in a corner of his mouth, and halted it when he was still a quarter of a mile from town. He studied the clustered adobes of Durango through his field glasses. The town was too quiet . . . it looked deserted.

He turned and called a lieutenant to his side. "Take a half dozen men," he ordered. "Scout the town. Find out why the *jefe*, Camillo, isn't coming out to meet us."

The lieutenant saluted. He picked out six men . . . they rode toward Durango.

Cobb Eaton watched them come. He had not counted on this. He wondered if it might not be better to let this advance patrol enter the town. Then—

But Avilla had given strict orders. *Hold Durango!*

He said calmly: "Well, this is it. We'll wait until they're within range. Don't miss!"

The patrol rode at a jog toward Durango. When they were within a hundred yards the Americans fired. All seven men were killed in that first volley. . . .

Watching, General Franco clamped his teeth down hard on his cigar.

"All right," he said harshly, "no quarter . . ."

He relayed orders to his guns. Quickly and efficiently they wheeled the artillery pieces around, muzzles pointing toward Durango.

The first volley was high, exploding into the buildings behind the Americans.

As the gunners reloaded, the troopers flanked out, prepared to charge. . . .

Avilla and Tomas were already mounted . . . they gave a command signal and the hundred eager men swept out of the gully and charged the Mexican column.

It should have worked. General Franco was caught by surprise and for a moment his line of command was thrown into confusion.

Then the confusion swept back into the ranks of the

charging revolutionaries as the shiny new rifles they had waited so long for did not fire.

For every *Amigo* whose Winchester fired there were four which did not.

The veteran troopers from Mexico City rallied and charged the suddenly confused and helpless revolutionaries—who broke and tried now only to escape. Methodically and efficiently the troopers shot them down . . . chasing them back into the gully.

Tomas was killed at the first volley, clutching a rifle that didn't work. He died turning to look at Avilla, a shocked and bitter question in his eyes—a question Avilla could not answer, had no time to answer . . .

He fired his weapon and kept firing, but he knew his cause was lost, and he cursed Cass Borman wildly, knowing in these final tragic moments how he had been betrayed.

The rifle bullet hit him in the stomach and went through him . . . he felt the burn of it like a red hot poker in his insides and he fell forward, losing his rifle, clutching at his horse's mane. The animal was running wildly now, heading for the hills.

All around him men were falling, yelling . . . horses ran by without riders. Avilla hung on, only half conscious, thinking of Borman . . . there was only one terrible thought left in his mind. He wanted to stay alive . . . he wanted to live just long enough to get his hands around Cass Borman's neck. . . .

General Franco sat his horse and watched the slaughter without expression, the cigar clamped firmly in a corner of his mouth. The artillery was lobbing shells toward Durango . . . he ordered them to cease firing.

He shook his head. A rabble, he thought—nothing but a rabble. He looked toward the town which was now strangely quiet.

His troopers re-formed . . . their losses against Avilla had been extremely light.

At Franco's signal they rode into Durango. The ten men trapped in the town never had a chance. . . .

XVII

FROM HIGH up in the desert hills Jeff and Roger viewed the battle for Durango . . . it seemed an unreal, distant stage play of toy soldiers and barely heard crackling of rifles. The heavier explosions of the artillery were like hollow poppings punching through the dying day.

They witnessed the rout of Avilla and his men, although neither Jeff nor Roger could understand why it had failed so dismally. And when the Mexican troopers under General Franco re-formed and went charging into Durango, Jeff and Roger turned and rode away.

They camped that night somewhere north of Durango, on a slope just above a deep and rock-strewn arroyo. There were clouds gathering in the south, moving toward them, and Jeff knew the desert country well enough to know what a flash flood roaring down that arroyo could do. Rain came suddenly here, and in torrents, and, sometimes, even when the sun was shining. The land was gullied and torn and constantly being reshaped . . . it was the same land that ran up into western Texas and Arizona and New Mexico . . . dry and forbidding and sparsely populated.

They rested around a small fire of *piñon* nuts and branches. Neither felt very hungry, but in any case they had nothing to eat. Jeff was thankful for the canteen Nogales had fastened to the mule's saddle.

Roger's back and right shoulder had stiffened. He lay with his head pillowed on a saddle, a folded blanket under his back to ease the discomfort . . . he watched Jeff hunkered down by the fire, the flames outlining the ex-Ranger's hard face. The blood had dried around the bullet cut on Jeff's arm—if it bothered him he did not show it.

"I've seen you before," Roger said. "You're not Galahad. Who are you?"

Jeff shrugged. "Jeff Corrin."

"Corrin?" Roger's brow knitted in thought. "I met a Texas Ranger named Corrin—"

"My brother Ben," Jeff said shortly. He tossed a couple of *piñon* nuts on the fire. "He was waiting for me in Ansara. I was to help him find out what happened to you. He was killed before I got there."

"Borman?"

"Borman was there," Jeff replied, "sending a wire

story to your paper, in your name. But it was Gordon who killed Ben. That's what Nogales said."

Roger nodded. "Of course." He looked at Jeff, interested. "Is that why you came into Mexico?"

Jeff thought a moment before replying. "My brother wanted me back in the Rangers. I . . ." He paused, thinking back. "I was just drifting . . ."

Roger said: "I remember now. You were a Ranger once— I think I remember reading about a trial . . ." He waited for Jeff to say something, but Jeff was looking into the fire. The memories Roger had recalled were not pleasant.

"What happened to Gordon?"

"I killed him," Jeff said. He did not elaborate, but added: "I guess the others are dead, too . . ."

"So is George Taine," Roger said. He saw by the way Jeff turned his head and looked at him that Jeff had not known.

"I heard Borman tell Maria. He killed Taine—or had him killed . . ." Roger paused and shifted his weight slightly, trying to ease his sore back.

"I'm sorry to hear about Taine," Jeff said. "He knew who I was, the moment he drove into the *Paseo Grande* yard. One word from him—" He took a long breath, staring into the campfire. "I think he knew then that Borman would kill him. He was practically a prisoner on his own ranch . . . he told me as much . . . and there was nothing I could do to help . . ."

Roger's voice was bitter: "Looks like Cass Borman won it all."

"Looks like it." Jeff stood up and gazed off into the darkness. "He's probably headed back for the *Paseo Grande* . . ."

He turned back to Roger. "You wouldn't know how to get back there, would you?" The newspaperman grinned at the thought. Jeff saw the look on his face and smiled. "I don't, either. But maybe in the morning I can pick up their tracks. Borman can't be too far ahead of us . . ."

Roger looked up at the stars, thinking. "The *Paseo Grande* won't be worth much to Borman, now that Taine is dead and Avilla and his *Amigos* wiped out. But the Triangle T would—"

He looked at Jeff, frowning. "I wonder why he came all the way to Durango for Maria?"

Jeff thought of the girl then, and said simply: "Some men want most what they can't get. . . ."

Vincente Avilla rested through the hours of the night, curled up like a desert animal, one hand pressed to the hole in his stomach which now oozed only a little blood. The other was wrapped around the reins of his horse. He couldn't risk letting the animal get away from him—he knew he was dying . . . knew it was only a matter of time.

He prayed, looking up at the stars . . . he prayed for a chance to get to Borman before he slipped away into that distant eternity. At times he was delirious and thought he was riding again at the head of the *Amigos* . . . he called out sharply: "Tomas . . . ho,

Tomas!" and his horse, startled, moved away, dragging him several yards before Avilla came to and stopped him.

He slept fitfully after that, but the fever seemed to pass from his brain . . . when dawn stained the eastern horizon he dragged himself up into the saddle. He was chilled . . . he shivered as much from weakness, however, as from the desert cold.

He gazed up at the stars beginning to dim in the sky, getting his bearings by them—he knew which way to go to get to the *Paseo Grande*. That's where he was headed. He thought Cass Borman was still there.

Maria?

She came to his mind then and he almost turned back to Durango. She had always been with him for the revolution—and she had come with him to Durango. But he knew that nothing he could possibly do now could help her . . . he could only pray that General Franco would be lenient with her.

He took a small swallow of water from his canteen. His wound was still oozing blood . . . he knew he had only a limited time left. He slid his hand down the cold butt plate of his holstered gun and prayed for enough time to get to Borman.

The horse under him snorted as he turned north toward the distant *Paseo Grande*. . . .

Jeff Corrin and Roger were moving in an almost identical path, although Jeff was not so sure that he was headed in the right direction. This was new country to him and although he tried to recognize landmarks, he knew that a mesa or a peak or even a jumble of rocks looked one way when approached from one direction and another when viewed from the opposite side.

He had not paid much attention to the trail from *Paseo Grande* to the abandoned village of Santa Lucia and finally to Durango because at that time he had not considered coming back this way.

But now he was being forced into reconsidering his position. He had avenged Ben's murder, but he had not finished Ben's job . . . it wouldn't be finished until he brought Cass Borman back across the border into Texas to stand trial in an American court.

For Borman had killed his brother Ben as surely as Gordon, who had pulled the trigger.

It was Roger who worried about Maria.

"Maybe that's why Borman came to Durango for her," he said, during a morning break. "Maybe, at first, he wanted her that badly. But—" He paused to reflect, pulling together what he knew of the man who had held him prisoner. "The way things stand now, with George Taine dead, he'll take over the Triangle T. That's where the money is, and the power. The *Paseo Grande* can't be held . . . the Mexican authorities know pretty well by now where Vince Avilla's support came from.

"He can get by with almost any story, once he gets into Texas . . . everyone knows of the trouble in northern Mexico . . . he could just say he was lucky to get back across the border alive . . .

"But if he takes Maria with him he'll have to share the Triangle T with her. And he'll never be sure she won't go to the district attorney with the real story of what happened . . . he'll never be sure of her—"

Jeff cut in: "You think he'll kill her?"

Roger shrugged. "He may be thinking that way now." He looked grim. "Borman's gotten everything he wanted, even Maria, so far—but he may be thinking he doesn't want her that much now . . ."

Jeff looked off into the long glaring reaches of desert ahead. Jagged hills ran like a sawtooth barrier across it.

Borman and his men could be somewhere just ahead . . . *but where?*

"I could get you back across the border," he told Roger. "But if we go after Borman—?"

He left it up to the newspaperman.

Roger tried to move his shoulder . . . it was stiff and it pained him. He smiled uncertainly. "I don't want to be a hero," he said slowly . . . "I'd much rather head straight for Texas. But—" he looked off, his news-paperman's mind working—"if we get Cass Borman, I'll have the story of a lifetime. . . ."

XVIII

BORMAN WAS camped in an old Mexican peasant's hut—
a goat herder's place, abandoned when revolutionary unrest swept across this part of Mexico. A few of the goats
still came back, for the small spring back of the stone
and adobe hut was the only water for miles around.

The horse Maria had been riding had gone lame . . .
somehow it had thrown a hind shoe during the early
morning hours and the land they were crossing was
hard on unshod hoofs. And, too, the canteen which had
hung from Maria's saddle had disappeared . . . thinking about it now, Borman suspected that she had
been the cause of both annoyances.

Not that Borman was in a hurry. He wasn't figuring
on pursuit.

Brazos Red was dozing in the shade of the hut, his
hat pulled down over his eyes, his back against the wall.
He slept with his gloved hand resting on his gun butt
. . . and he slept lightly, stirring at once as Borman took
a step toward him.

The other two men were by a small campfire. Gabe
Beaver, some fifty years old and whang leather tough
was boiling water for coffee. He claimed to have been
a mountain man with Fremont—Borman knew him as
a liar and a cold-blooded killer. Gabe carried a hunt-

ing knife in a sheath at his belt—it had been he who had killed Camillo and his wife, with as little compunction as though he had been slitting the throat of a chicken.

Bill Gunning, the other man with Gabe, picking at his teeth, was younger by more than twenty years. He was a dull-witted man, so-so with a gun, but dependable.

Both men had been among the first Borman had hired on at the *Paseo Grande*.

He watched them for a long moment, like a man contemplating pawns on a chess board. And, like pawns, he figured they were expendable.

Nor, he reflected cold-bloodedly, did he need Maria. He had always been a man more occupied with other things than women . . . he took them, when it occurred to him, casually, his mind often on other things.

Maria had gotten to him because she was the most feminine woman he had seen in a long, long time—but mostly because she had always held him off. He had wanted her because he couldn't have her. Looking at her now, resting in the shade of a small *ramada*, he realized how dangerous it would be to take her with him into Texas.

He thought about this for a moment and then went inside the hut and picked up his rifle. It had been a long time since he had done his own killing.

He came to the doorway and looked toward Gabe . . . neither he nor Gunning noticed Borman. Brazos

Red was still dozing . . . Maria was staring off toward the near hills.

Borman raised his rifle and killed Gabe with his first shot. The man fell across the fire, spilling the coffee pot . . . fire licked up and around his body.

Gunning turned, a stunned look on his dull face. Borman's next shot spun him around. He fell, clawed the earth and the next shot snuffed out his life.

Borman lowered his rifle and looked into the muzzle of Brazos' gun.

"Put that away, Red," he said calmly.

Brazos came to his feet, the gun still leveled at Borman. He said: "You gone crazy?"

Borman glanced at Maria, who had come to her feet —she was staring at them, a hundred feet away.

Borman said almost casully: "No—just smart." He started to raise his rifle at Maria and Brazos snapped:
"Hold it, Cass!"

Borman said: "We don't need Gabe and Bill any more—we don't need her, either. With her out of the way I own all of the Triangle T—"

"And me?" Brazos cut in grimly. "Where do I fit in?"

"I need a man to help me run it," Borman said. He smiled placatingly. "Just you and me, making it across the border. Mexican bandits got the rest . . . including the girl . . . who'll question us, Red?"

He turned around again, his rifle leveling—but Maria was already on the run, heading toward the hills. Cass fired hurriedly, annoyed at his carelessness at having taken the time to talk to Brazos. He missed with the first shot, but the second staggered Maria . . . she kept running, however, and disappeared into one of the innumerable erosion gullies that spider-webbed the dry land.

Borman was not too concerned. He reloaded without hurry. The smell of burning flesh wafted to him and he said: "Get Gabe out of there," to Brazos.

Brazos considered for a moment before obeying. The offer Borman had extended appealed to him, but he knew he would always have to be wary of this man.

He went over and pulled Gabe's body out of the fire and beat out the flames.

Borman said: "Saddle the horses. She's hurt—she can't get too far . . ."

He waited, watching Brazos, the rifle resting in the crook of his arm. *Getting rusty,* he thought . . . *once he could have killed her with his first shot. . . .*

Drooped over his horse's neck, Avilla heard the first rifle shots . . . he forced himself erect, fighting the grayness that was inexorably creeping into his brain.

He had been drifting this way—how long he wasn't sure. But the shots—?

He was at the base of a rocky slope, looking off across a baked plain . . . he could see someone running toward him—and someone else, in front of a stone hut standing alone on a desolate plain, firing again. The running figure disappeared, but he recognized the man who had been firing . . . savagely he dug his spurs into his horse's flanks, sent him lunging toward the goat herder's shack.

A half mile east of Avilla, Jeff and Roger were riding down a wide wash. Jeff had earlier come across the tracks of five horses—they were recent and he felt they had to be Borman's party.

The rifle shots alerted him. He stood up in his stirrups and could just see over the bank of the wash . . . the goat herder's shack was less than a quarter of a mile away.

He recognized Maria, running . . . she disappeared, and then he saw Borman and Brazos Red mount and ride after her.

He drew his rifle and sent his horse lunging up the bank, not waiting for Roger Briscole. . . .

Avilla reached Maria first. She had staggered up out of the gully as he rode up . . . he saw her through a red haze and he did not even have time to be surprised. Up ahead, Cass Borman, riding in front of Brazos Red, pulled to a sudden stop, stark amazement on his face.

Avilla drew and fired. His shot killed Borman's horse. Borman went down with the animal and Avilla kept firing as he rode toward the man momentarily pinned under his mount . . . he emptied his gun at Borman—missing him in his haste, his desperation.

Borman pulled free and started to run . . . Avilla swept up beside him and lunged out of his saddle, his hands going for Borman's throat. They went down together and he was still on top of Borman when Brazos Red killed him.

Maria screamed.

Brazos swung around to her, his gun leveling . . . he jerked and fired quickly as he saw Jeff Corrin, seemingly coming out of nowhere, riding toward him. He fired again—Jeff's horse stumbled and Jeff rolled out of his saddle, Red's bullets kicking up sand around him. Jeff steadied himself briefly and fired at Brazos.

The gunman doubled . . . he dropped his Colt and then tried to pick it up . . . he died a few moments later, lying doubled over his gun, on the hot, baked earth.

Borman rolled free of Avilla's body only to find himself looking into Jeff's leveled gun. Behind Jeff he could see another rider coming toward them . . . a few moments later he recognized Roger Briscole.

He had it all, he thought numbly—*and had lost it all.*

Maria was kneeling over Avilla's body, crying . . . she looked up at Jeff.

"Galahad . . ." she said brokenly, "how . . . ?"

"The name's Corrin," he said quietly, "Jeff Corrin." He looked at Borman. "It's a long story, Maria . . . I'll tell it to you later . . . on the way back to Texas . . ."

They buried Vincente Avilla where he died, and where he would have wanted to be buried, on the parched and desolate plains of Mexico. They marked it with a wooden cross Jeff made from wood from the goat herder's hut. Brazos Red, Gabe and Gunning were buried in a wash behind the shack.

Borman rode with his hands tied behind his back—ahead of Jeff and Roger. Maria rode between them . . . quiet, grieving. Her wound was slight; it was a deeper hurt that numbed her. In time the pain would ease . . . the pain of a revolution betrayed . . . dreams killed. But she would never forget.

The four of them moved out across that desolate land . . . they rode north, toward Texas.